A Tale of Two Djinns

MINA KHAN

A Letter to the Reader

Thank you for buying this book and helping me support a cause close to my heart—literacy. I have pledged to donate fifty percent of the proceeds from the sale of A Tale of Two Djinns to UNICEF's new Schools for Asia initiative.

Everything I am today is thanks to my parents, and education is one of the best gifts they gave me. Thanks to my education, I discovered my love of reading and writing, pursued an adventurous journalism career, and became a published author.

Growing up in Bangladesh, I have seen the poorest of poor. I have seen children forced to work instead of attending school. I have also seen education make a difference —lead to job opportunities, raise the quality of life for entire families, and allow individuals new possibilities.

Unfortunately, many don't get this precious education. According to UNICEF, 67 million children are currently not enrolled in school worldwide, and 26 million of them live in the Asia-Pacific Region. How much potential is the world losing out on? How many Einsteins, Joyce Carol Oateses, and more remain undiscovered because they were born in bad circumstances?

My mother never finished high school. Back in the early 1950s, in traditional Bangladesh where arranged marriages were the norm and good proposals a blessing, my mother was married to a handsome young sailor. She was seventeen and he was nineteen. Her father, who had great hopes for his clever eldest child, agreed to the marriage only after the groom's father promised to let her continue her studies. This promise was not kept.

Many years later, older and wiser, my mother insisted on her daughters being educated, finishing college. Her favorite saying is "No one can take knowledge away from you." My late father, who knew a thing or two about raising daughters, made our education a family priority.

Today I'm passing forward the gift of education—with your help—through UNICEF's Schools for Asia, which will be working in Bangladesh, Bhutan, China, India, Lao PDR, Mongolia, Nepal, Papua New Guinea, Philippines, Timor-Leste, and Vietnam. I hope together we will make a difference.

Thank you for your support, and I hope you enjoy the story!

Mina Khan

DEDICATION

For my Dad, the late great Capt. Rashid Khan,
who knew a thing or two about raising daughters and
shared his love of adventure with me. For my Mom,
Sufia, who insisted on my education and fueled me with
her fierce determination.

ACKNOWLEDGMENTS

This story exists because of many kind people: my wonderful critique partner Lucie J. Charles, Anne Leslie Tuttle of Harlequin for feedback, my invaluable beta readers Joya, Mary, Adrienne and Alisha, the very supportive LL ladies & lads, editing helpmate Anne, and my encouraging readers. Last, but not least, my Darling Husband without whose love, support and patience none of this would ever happen.

.

PROLOGUE

All wars end in defeat.

Prince Akshay stood on a hilltop and watched the sun rise as he chewed on a piece of dry Ibir-grain bread to settle his churning gut. The early light bathed the waiting battlefield rosy, illuminated the dark and twisty thorn vines choking the mouth of Nijhoom Forest.

Dew-wet grass prickled the soles of his feet as he closed his eyes and concentrated until he could hear the earth breathe, the soft rush of the wind, and the whispers of the dead. So many soldiers had stood and died on this very ground.

Memory after memory skittered past like dead leaves, and whispers full of desire and despair clawed him from all sides, scraped him raw. Akshay gritted his teeth and wished he could shut out the swirl of voices. Unfortunately, an earth djinn could only hear the song the soul of the world chose to sing. He poured more of his strength into his will and listened harder, deeper.

Below the overwhelming whispers, he detected a softer refrain, woven through with promise and hope. A faint stirring of life as the liquid dew soaked into the parched ground, a gentle crackle of energy from seeds lying dormant and hidden in the dark. Beyond it all, lay the weighty deep pulsing heartbeat of the earth.

Akshay dropped to all fours, kissed the ground and said a prayer.

A silent squadron of birds, black silhouettes against the lurid sky, flew overhead. Behind him rose a soft symphony of men calling to each other, nervous whinnies of horses, and the creak and clang of armor and weapons in the camp.

The gnawing emptiness in the pit of his stomach grew and reminded him the enemy would arrive with full daylight. Along with death.

If only there'd been another way.

Impatient familiar footsteps, accompanied by the metal-on-metal scrape of armor, alerted him to the approach of his chief bodyguard and childhood friend, Patthar Dar Muth. Akshay pulled on his socks and boots and straightened.

A heavy sigh floated into the morning breeze as Patthar stopped next to him. "Do you really think there is a land blessed with rivers and streams on the other side of this arboreal monster?"

The forest did look monstrous and foreboding, the stretch of plain in front held nothing but dried brown grass and some skeletal shrubs. As daylight bleached color from the sky, even the air grew hot and arid. No hint of life-giving waters.

The prince shrugged. "No one has seen the land of waters for centuries, but the legends describe it and the elders believe it exists."

"It'd be a shame to risk life and limb for the sake of a fairytale."

Akshay's gaze slid over his soldiers gearing up for battle. Lots of lives and limbs were at stake. But the elders insisted every prince had to prove himself with an attempt to get water from the water djinns before he could be declared heir. All he had to do was put in a good effort and stay alive.

Victory and water, the real prizes, were both as elusive as a desert mirage. Many had tried and failed, but enough survived to become rulers of the earth djinns. Now it was his turn. "Good of you to wake up in time for battle."

"Hey, I have my priorities straight," Patthar said. "The sooner we take care of this, the sooner we can get back to the human dimension and what's important. Babes, beer and barbecue!"

Akshay barked out a laugh as he shook his head. Patthar loved being among humans so much, their slang poured off his tongue with ease. "How can you think of women and food at a time like this?"

"Why not?" Patthar shrugged. "I'd rather think of the pleasures life offers, than worry about death." He held out Akshay's helmet, the plume of peacock feathers dancing in the breeze. "You forgot this in the tent."

"Thank you." The prince turned to his friend, studied the rough-hewn face and dark eyes glimmering with mischief, then grabbed the helmet from him. "Sometimes, my friend, you say the wisest things."

Patthar's eyes widened as if he'd just been sentenced to torture. "Heaven and hell! That must be remedied ASAP. Wise is for old men, I'm still a young rogue."

"Fine, let's survive the battle first, and then I'll help bolster your reputation by buying drinks at your favorite human bar."

"Party at the Lonesome Cowboy," Patthar grinned. "I'll hold you to that."

"I'll be happy to deliver." He'd like nothing better than to escape into the parallel human dimension. The smoky, dark bar would be more welcome than this morning-washed battlefield. The prince narrowed his eyes at the sky. Only a streak of pink clouds remained. He checked his armor and broadsword fastening, then settled the metal helmet on his skull and picked up his heavy shield. "Ready?"

"Let's go kick some water djinn ass."

As they strode forward, kicking up dust with every step, horns bellowed calling the soldiers to assemble. Akshay winced, even though there was no point in maintaining silence. The enemy knew they were there. Somehow they always did.

The five remaining members of his royal guard rode up and joined them as a horsekeeper ran forward with Midnight. Akshay had raised the pitch black mount from a colt. A deep whiff of Midnight's musky scent—like sun-warmed earth—slowed some of the tension curdling in his gut, transformed it into battle-ready calm. He swung into the saddle and looked over at Patthar, who now sat on his own dapple gray steed. What better way to go into battle but be carried by a friend, and have another at his side? He wheeled Midnight around to face his troops.

Sunlight glinted off metal helmets and body armor, off staffs and bows and spears. First came the horse cavalry, behind them the foot soldiers and charioteers carrying the archers. The last line of attack, his last resort weapon, were the molewyrms—giant earthworm-mole creatures carrying metal capsules occupied by drivers and additional archers. They wore blinders to protect their sensitive eyes from daylight, but once the creatures burrowed into earth, they were unstoppable.

Quiet pride warmed Akshay as he surveyed his men. The earth djinns would much prefer to farm the land and bring forth gifts from the soil, but they were master of all earth and earth-creatures. They could work metal and stone into the best weapons, and had the skill to wield them too.

"This day we are gathered to fight, not for fame, glory or riches, but for life." His unrelenting gaze touched face after face. "Water is life. The Creator's gift, meant for one and all. Yet the water djinns hoard it. We have every right to fight for our fair share. Are you with me?"

"Yes! Yes! Yes!" A thousand feet stamping the earth at the same time accompanied the resounding cry. The strength and resonance of their voices filled Akshay with hope.

"I ask you to fight not for the Royal House of Zammen. Not for the Kingdom of Bhramadesh. But for your children and grandchildren."

Eyes, staring back, glittered with fierce light.

"Think of fields of golden wheat and fruit orchards heavy with fruit. Think of the legacy you want to leave behind."

A soft rustle spread through the ranks as spines straightened and shoulders squared.

"Are you with me, Djinns of the Earth?"

"Yes! Yes! Yes!" Another stamp of feet.

"May the Creator be merciful to us and our enemies."

"Amen! Amen! Amen!" came the resounding reply.

He kicked Midnight into a run and thundered to the front. Patthar, grinning madly, rode at his shoulder. Together they descended the hill, their advance shaking the earth. In front, the dark woods stood silent and still.

The enemy emerged from the forest like wisps of mist, and then solidified into translucent wraith-like creatures that flew fast toward the plain. Long, tortured moans shivered in the air, turning Akshay's blood ice cold. At his side, Patthar let out a yell full of rage. The earth djinns picked it up until their roar drowned all else.

As the two armies drew closer, many of the water djinns morphed into rhakshas. Akshay almost slipped from his horse as the ugly brutes materialized. Damn, the overused cloaking trick.

Rhakshas, nomadic mercenaries, preferred the old-style look—tall and broad like giants, they sported bald heads, teeth like elephant tusks and huge glowing red eyes. He much preferred the current trend of humanoid appearances. Unfortunately, their fighting skills were as ferocious as their looks. How much water had it taken to bribe desert folk to switch sides?

"Stay behind," Patthar shouted, drawing his long sword and galloping forward.

"Yeah right," Akshay muttered and rushed Midnight to the front with his own weapon ready. A wraith came at him like a whirlwind, flashing a lot of steel. Others followed.

Soon the metallic clang of clashing weapons and the screams of those wounded or dying filled the air. Sweat burned his eyes as Akshay hacked and slashed his way through water wraiths and solid rhakshas.

He chanced a quick look at the sky. Lava bombs and fiery arrows flew overhead toward the forest. His archers were following the plan. As the first tree top burst into flame, Akshay let out a soft "Yes!"

Thunder rumbled in the distant sky, followed by hard, fast rain. It fell in dense curtains that obscured vision, melted the ground at their feet into soft mud, and put out the precious fire. Damn water djinns! Thank the Creator, they were fighting on dry land rather than by an ocean.

Mudslide. Akshay jumped from Midnight's back and landed in the mud. As his feet sank into the soft, wet mess, he wrested control of the earth, twisted and turned it to his command.

A howling rhaksha leapt out of a skidding slide and landed in front of him swinging a scimitar. Akshay managed to duck and miss the blow. How could such ungainly beasts move so fast?

Finding an opening, the Prince thrust his sword and buried it to the hilt in the rhaksha's gray flesh.

"Shay!"

He spun around, weapon ready, at the warning.

A man, his face covered in an assassin's black mask, held a dagger mere inches from his face. Breath caught painfully in Akshay's throat for a long moment. Then the man crumpled into his swirling black robes and dropped to the ground, revealing Patthar holding a bloody sword.

Before he could take a breath to thank Patthar, a second figure hidden in a flowing black hooded robe materialized behind his friend. Assassins. A thin flash of silver winked in the air, and Patthar's head separated from his body.

Akshay's insides quivered and turned liquid. A scream lodged in his throat—soundless and ineffectual—as his friend's body tumbled to the ground in a splatter of blood. Patthar's head rolled in the mud and stopped, thankfully facing away from him.

Gathering himself, Akshay lunged at the assassin. Adrenaline surged through him as his blade touched the murderer's throat. He thrust with all his strength only to meet empty air. The figure dissipated into the wind like flecks of ash and disappeared.

The water djinns had stooped so low as to hire air assassins? For a battle? Did they have no honor? Rage surged inside like molten lava, fluid and hot, wanting to flatten, burn, and bury the enemy.

An army of dense gray clouds covered the dawn sky, silver lightning flashed and crackled among them like demented swords. Akhsay's gaze met the red burning eyes of a rhaksha.

He charged, sending a barrage of stones hurtling in front, hewing out a path to the beast. The thing's stink made Akshay gag as the distance closed between them.

With a battle cry, the prince threw himself into the fight with the creature, each going for blood and death. The clang of blades and grunts charged the air. Finally they struggled hand-to-hand and weapons tangled.

Akshay gritted his teeth and pressed his blade down. The rhaksha trembled and half-sank into the mud, all the while pushing back with its scimitar. He stared into the beast's blood red eyes, willing it to give up and die.

The rhaksha yelled in his face and shoved hard.

Choking on the swampy stink of its breath, Akshay stumbled back. The two stood breathing hard, eyes locked. Icy rain lashed the prince's face and hands, sharp and stinging, like loss stung his heart.

Patthar had died protecting him, now the water djinns would pay.

Akshay threw back his head and released his anger into the wind. A raw, primal roar ripped out from deep inside, charged from his throat. He called the molewyrms with vengeance.

Thunder roared back in answer. Rain spattered his skin like tears. The ground beneath his feet shook. What started as a faint tremble broke into bone-shuddering quakes. The earth split its seams and spat out mud balls and stone.

The rhaksha lurched in place, eyes wide with fear. Akshay leapt forward, slicing down with his sword.

With an ear-piercing howl, the mountain of ugly fell backward, landed with a wet splat. The air around the creature wavered and reality hiccupped. Instead of an ungainly rhaksha, a most uncommon woman lay in the mud.

A female in the battlefield? What the hell? Breath rushed out of Akshay. He twisted his descending blade at the last second so that it sliced through the fleshy part of her right arm instead of her throat. A muted cry of pain escaped from between her full lips.

Silver armor, like glittering fish scales, covered her head and slim body and, damn, she had legs that just kept going. Double damn, he'd always been a leg man. His gaze jerked back up and met terrified whiskey-colored eyes set in an elfin face of the most delicate blue of a robin's egg.

Tremors wracked the battlefield as more molewyrms tore out of the ground. One appeared so near that a shower of mud covered Akshay from head to toe. When he'd wiped the grime off his face, the woman had vanished.

Akshay staggered and cursed. The damn creatures were supposed to go past the battlefield and emerge in the Waterlands, or at least in the water djinn camp. Not in the middle of the battle.

The air thickened as howling wraiths fled toward the forest. Both earth djinns and rhakshas slipped and slid in the mud trying to escape.

He ran at the nearest molewyrm, shouting at the driver to lower the rope ladder. Akshay snagged the swinging ladder and pulled himself up against cool, moist molewyrm skin as chaos wreaked havoc below.

Soldiers on both sides fell, got trampled beneath panicked feet and smothered by uncaring molewyrms. Screams, curses and prayers filled the air until Akshay longed to cover his ears. Instead, he held on for dear life and watched the last of the wraiths melt into the dark trees. The rope ladder cut into his skin. The destruction didn't stop until all fifty of the creatures he'd brought to the battle had emerged from the earth and stood with their noses quivering.

The hot, metallic stench of blood soaked the air and made his stomach pitch. With a hiss, Akshay unclenched his bleeding fists and dropped to the ground. What a freaking disaster.

CHAPTER ONE

Almost dying served as a heck of a reminder to take care of unfinished business. Unfortunately, her Aunt Denidra had decided to drive home the message with a hammer.

Maya sat on the hospital cot, studying her bandaged arm as the tall, willowy Royal Mage paced the floor, her boots echoing across the wood. "You could have died out there."

Wow, really? Duh. She'd been the one battling the crazy earth djinn. Maya cleared her throat and looked up. "Back there, I felt a sudden suck of magic from me and around me. What happened?"

Denidra's purple eyes narrowed as she threw up her hands. "Those damn earthworm creatures attacked," she said. "I had to divert more power to strengthen the underground fortifications. I have never seen such giant bits of ugliness before."

The leak in power had made Maya lose control of the illusion. While manipulation of water came easy to water djinns, working with witch power—true magic inherited from a powerful human ancestor—came with more challenges.

"Did the *earthslug* see you?"

Maya knew Denidra referred to the djinn warrior and not the creatures. "Maybe."

The djinn's dark, glittering eyes had burned at her through the opening of his helmet, almost searing her with their focus. Welded her to the spot. "It all happened so fast." She shrugged. "Then one of those worms was between us and I just got out of there."

"Probably the best course of action under the circumstances." With a sigh, Denidra sat on the cot and smoothed Maya's hair away from her face. "I'm just glad you're okay."

"Aww, Aunt Denidra." Maya threw her arms around her aunt and mentor. "I love you too."

"You can just drop the aunt bit. Stop aging me," Denidra said, laying her head on top of Maya's. "And you're still not off the hook."

The door slid open and the queen of the water djinns entered with a soft swish of silk. Her worried gaze latched onto Maya. Great, now she'd get lectured in stereo.

"I'm fine, Mom. Really."

Her mother rushed to her side and stroked the other side of her face. "That's good to know."

Denidra arched an eyebrow. "I was just reminding my niece about her neglected duty."

"Sorry, I was busy training our warriors," Maya said. "I think having a strong defense is somewhat important to our country." Damn, she'd so wanted to avoid this talk. Somehow dealing with weapons came easier than dealing with men. Weapons didn't complicate things.

The queen sat down, deftly trapping her between the two women.

"Yes, but so is continuity." Denidra said. "You're of royal blood—"

Maya interrupted her aunt. "And Sidha has already produced an heir and stand-in heirs."

The sisters glared at her. The queen cleared her throat. "We are not referring to that kind of heirs."

Denidra sniffed. "You're of royal blood and one of the few females carrying the witch ability," she said. "It is your duty to pass on the gene to protect not only the country, but our freedom."

Her mother patted her arm. "There are so many families offering for your hand, all you'd have to do is choose a male who pleases you."

Yeah, she wasn't under any illusion as to why. Even though she was merely a minor princess, one of seven, she was still a princess. Any of the local families would jump to establish ties to the royal family. She wouldn't put up with someone who only wanted her for her pedigree.

"Oh, for the love of the Creator." Maya fell back onto the cot and stared at the thatched ceiling. "Did we get taken over by the chauvinistic earth djinns while I wasn't looking?"

"Maya!" Her mother's voice upped a notch. "Don't even joke about that."

"You're the one telling me to marry out of duty," she said. "I thought a woman had freedom to live as she pleased among the water djinns in Shagaard."

Maya had long ago accepted marriage and happily-ever-after weren't for her. She was useful on the training grounds and battlefield...and happy.

"Who said you have to marry?" Denidra countered. "Just get pregnant."

A coughing fit took over the queen. Denidra rushed to the pitcher on the small table next to the cot and poured out a glass of water. "Here, don't die on me."

The queen gulped in air and water, and then cleared her throat. "Marriage isn't all bad. I quite enjoy being married to your father, most days," she said. "But Denidra is correct."

With a groan, Maya slapped her palms over her face. Was she truly having this conversation with her mother and aunt? "Fine," she said. "I'll put sex on the top of my to-do list."

"Good," Denidra said. "Now you can't procreate with just anybody! He has to be virile, strong, disease-free—"

"It'd be so much easier if you'd just let us preselect candidates," her mother interrupted.

Maya groaned again. She wanted to stick her fingers in her ears and sing "La-la-la!" as loud as possible. "Oh, Creator, my head is killing me," she said. "I need some sleep and quiet."

"Of course, you should get some rest," the queen shot off the bed. "We'll start working on the list." The two sisters hurriedly lowered all the blinds, throwing the room into soothing shadows. Maya sank deeper into her pillow, eyes half-closed. Being injured did have some advantages.

As the door shut behind them with a soft click, Maya let out a sigh. She was *not* going to let her mother meddle in her love life. She was definitely *not* going to get involved with a water djinn in Shagaard. Too many complications and politics.

An idea formed, followed by a grin. What she *was* going to do is head off to the human dimension and hook up with one of the loner djinns, preferably a hot and hunky one, who preferred to live outside the djinn dimension and had nothing to do with djinns and their politics. She could handle some no-strings-attached fun.

The Crowning of the Heir was pure torture and Akshay hated every minute of the two-hour ceremony.

One more moment in the Council Chambers under the bright glare of a thousand lamps, listening to the play-by-play recitation of his actions in battle, being stared at by everyone—from white-haired advisors to gaudily-dressed nobility—and Akshay would have hit someone.

Damn it, he didn't *feel* like a hero. All he'd accomplished was the death of Patthar and almost a thousand other earth djinns. The wink of silver slicing Patthar in two played through his mind, made him gag. All his years of training, all his warrior experience…useless.

Forced to walk behind his father, Akshay had to take measured regal steps. As soon as the heavy chamber doors shut behind them, cutting off the chatter of the crowd, he pulled off the gold pin featuring a sheaf of wheat—the Zammen royal family crest—and unbuttoned his collar. A long breath of relief whooshed out of him, earning Akshay amused looks from his father and his half-brother as they hurried down the carpeted corridor toward the Grand Ballroom for the reception.

"Better get used it dear brother, now that you're the Crown Prince," Jazzaz smirked. "Dressing up is part of the job. Plus, all the eligible young ladies will find you more appealing."

The blue woman swam to the surface of his thoughts. He'd never imagined a woman in armor, and now that glimpse haunted him. Soft woman and hard metal…unexpected and sexy as hell. Had she been real? Or was he losing his mind?

Akshay glared at Jazzaz. "You should have volunteered for the job then, seeing you're already such a dandy." The two brothers couldn't be more different. Where Akshay was bronzed by the sun, Jazzaz had skin as fair as the white sands of the eastern desert where his mother came from. Where Akshay loved the outdoors, Jazzaz was happiest at parties and balls.

"If you'd conveniently died a heroic death in battle, I would not have shirked my duty," Jazzaz returned. "As it is, I can best serve by advising you in yours."

"Boys, stop baiting each other." The king's arms went around his sons' shoulders. "You would both have been excellent choices. However, protocol says the first-born son must have the first opportunity. Just as protocol says the Crown Prince must dress up in stuffy clothes."

Jazzaz inclined his head. "Of course, we always bow to protocol."

King Ashok laughed and rumpled Jazzaz's carefully combed hair. "Protocols keep us civilized."

An old hollowness echoed in Akshay's gut as he glanced away from the two. His father ruled with absolute confidence. Jazz would too.

His brother didn't follow fashions, but set trends. He wielded words as easily as Akshay wielded a sword. Jazz would have been a better king—except for a birth order decided by fickle fate and protocol.

"Perhaps the protocol is wrong."

Two sets of unflinching gazes pinned him. The flickering flames of the wall sconces threw harsh shadows across their faces.

"I'm more comfortable on the battlefield, yet even there...I don't know if I really proved myself worthy." Akshay shrugged. "Jazz already knows many of the courtiers and ambassadors. He knows protocol and diplomacy."

King Ashok Dar Zammen stretched to his full height and folded his arms across his wide chest. "The council unanimously recognized that you made a worthy attempt on the battlefield," he said. "It wasn't your fault that the molewyrms ran into impenetrable walls underground and could go no further."

"Pah! Anything of the ground or in the ground should be ours to control." Akshay raked a hand through his hair. "I just don't understand it. That's why I think the council made a mistake."

"You dare doubt the generations of old wisdom of the collective council?" His father's eyes cooled and narrowed. "Instead of whining, be a man and do your duty."

Jazzaz slipped between the two of them, interrupting their glaring contest. He turned to Akshay and placed a hand on his arm. "Brother, I will always be there to help you. All you need do is ask."

Akshay smiled his first real smile in weeks. "Thanks."

The king pulled both men into a bone-crushing hug. "My boys."

A far door opened and their sister, Princess Ara, rushed toward them, her bangles and anklets clattering and chiming with every step like warning bells. "Hurry up! Ma says you're running late," she said. "The guests have already started arriving!"

"We are right behind you, daughter," Ashok said, releasing them. "Well gentlemen, we have our orders."

"Ah yes, the ladies are waiting." His brother smirked.

As Jazzaz fixed his hair, Akshay buttoned his collar and affixed the golden wheat sheaf back in place. "I'm thinking of taking a few days off to go to the human dimension."

"A vacation? Not a bad idea," his father said, tugging at the sleeves of his coat. "You've definitely earned it."

No, to mourn Patthar, but they didn't need to know that. His father wouldn't understand. He and his guards would journey to Pat's favorite place on earth, The Lonesome Cowboy, to remember their lost friend.

"When do you leave?" Jazzaz asked.

"First thing tomorrow."

CHAPTER 2

Maya stood across the street from the Lonesome Cowboy, pulling down the bottom of her short black tanktop. Denidra hovered at her side in the shadows. Every time the door swung open, soulful fiddle music spilled into the night air and men in cowboy hats and tight jeans sauntered in.

"We've watched long enough," whispered Denidra. "We're dressed to fit in and more men than women have entered."

Yeah, Maya liked the odds. All she had to do was walk into the place and start Night One of her plan. Her feet refused to move. "I want to be sure."

"Oh stop being a wuss," Denidra said. "You can face an enemy over swords, but you're scared shitless to walk into a bar and pick up a guy. Seriously?"

Maya's shoulders tightened. Why, oh why, had she let her aunt tag along?

"Because it's safer, I wanted to make sure you didn't wuss out, and this way you aren't stuck with your mother."

She rolled her eyes and sighed. Oh right, an aunt who had no compunction eavesdropping inside her head. Maya clutched the strap of her purse. Damn it, if she could pass for a giant rhaksha, she could certainly pull off horny female. "Let's go get it over with."

A man reached the door just before them. He tipped his hat and held the door open. "Evening, ladies."

"Thanks." Denidra smiled like a shark eyeing a fish buffet and batted her lashes. Maya swallowed the laugh tickling her throat. She'd chosen to start at a country bar, because the men generally had better manners than your average bar-type.

Several people, mostly men, stared as Maya hesitated for a moment at the neon-lit doorway. The saloon—or did this qualify as a joint?—was more crowded than she'd expected. Ignoring the rowdy bunch around the bucking mechanical bull, she focused herself. Her awareness thrummed with a pulsating mix of human and djinn energy…there were definitely some non-humans hanging out. She took a deep breath of smoky air and made her way across the peanut shell covered floor to the bar. Men smiled, gazes lingered, cowboy hats were tipped, and the sea of bodies parted. She hopped up on a leather barstool. Denidra climbed onto the next one.

The bartender shared an easy smile. "What would you like?"

"Two Shiner Bocks," she said.

"Comin' right up."

A scrawny, bow-legged man, who barely came up to her chest, sidled up. "So what's a nice girl like you doing in this hell hole?"

"Hey! Stop scaring customers away," the bartender said, placing the beer in front of Maya.

The man's blue eyes twinkled at her from a nest of laugh-lines. "I am a regular," he said. "You keep coming here and we'll get to be friends." He tipped his hat at her and ambled off.

The bartender grinned at her. "Johnny's about seventy, and harmless."

Maya nodded and took a swallow of beer, letting the cool, smooth bitterness momentarily drown her jitters.

"To beer, babes and barbecue!" The lusty cheer drew her attention to a group of clean shaven cowboys in the back near the pool tables. They laughed and drank around a table covered with a small army of beer bottles. Some even had giggling women in their laps.

She sensed their presence vibrate in the air. Djinns. Definite possibilities. If only she could giggle on demand, she might land herself a cozy lap. Too bad she'd never been a giggle-bunny. Her gaze shifted, and then collided with the dark, intense gaze of a cowboy silent in the group's midst. Breath stuck in her throat. *Breathe girl, breathe.*

His night-dark eyes stared at her from under thick, winged brows set in a tanned and chiseled face, beneath a black cowboy hat. He nursed a beer, aloof from everyone and everything, his gaze fixed on Maya. As if she alone existed. As if he could look inside her and read her soul.

The music from the jukebox, the chatter and laughter faded to a whisper. Her heart somersaulted in slow motion as heat rushed up her face. She dropped her gaze.

When she dared look again, he still lolled in his chair, half in the shadows, staring. Maya decided to match his bold stare and check him out.

A crisp white cotton shirt stretched across wide shoulders and a broad chest. Her gaze traveled up the thick, bronze column of his throat edged by dark hair that was a bit too long, bordering on shaggy. Stubble shadowed his rugged jaw, but didn't hide the dimple in his chin or the tempting lips that slowly curved into a half-smile.

Maya's gaze jerked up. *Those damned dark staring eyes.*

A hum of desire uncurled just beneath her breastbone and traveled south, settling warm and tingly between her legs.

The band started playing Pat Green's "Beer." Johnny bought a round of Shiner Bock in honor of the song and then asked Denidra for a dance. She leaned in close to Maya. "Go ask the cowboy for a dance."

"Which cowboy?"

"The one you've been checking out."

With a not-so-gentle nudge, Denidra slid from her stool and followed Johnny out to the dance floor.

Maya took a fortifying gulp of her new beer and glanced back at the table. The cowboy was gone. Her buzz dive-bombed. Shit. She bowed her head and sighed. Denidra was right. She needed to stop being a wuss. Now.

A tap on her shoulder had Maya swinging around. A cowboy with perfect white teeth and tousled blond hair stood next to her. Unfortunately, not *the* cowboy.

"Is that seat available?" he nodded at Denidra's recently vacated stool.

Cute, but no otherworldly vibrations of power. Definitely human. "My friend just went to dance," Maya said. "She'll be back."

"I'll keep her seat warm then." He slid onto the stool smooth as melted butter and stuck out his hand. "Name's Bo Harlan."

Oh-kay. Maya frowned. What would be the diplomatic way to tell him to get lost?

He folded his arms on the bar and grinned at her. "Let me buy you a drink."

"No thanks, I'm still working on mine."

"And I'm working on you." He nodded at the bartender. "Give the lady another Shiner."

"Don't." Maya turned back to the man, bristling. Forget gentle. "You're wasting your time cowboy, move on."

"Did I tell you I was a champion bull rider?" He grabbed his humungous silver buckle and jiggled it.

"So?"

"So I like a challenge." He leaned closer.

"And I like my men to last a whole lot longer than eight seconds."

"I can ride long and hard, baby," he said, leaning even closer. "Long and hard."

His boozy breath made Maya's stomach turn. She leaned away from him. Great, subtle and direct had both failed. Should she slam his head into the bar or toss her beer on him? Damn shame to waste good beer.

Damn it, he'd waited too long to make his move. Akshay cursed under his breath as the other cowboy leaned close to the gorgeous brunette. The flare of red hot jealousy edging his disappointment surprised him, propelled him forward.

The stiffening of her spine and the murderous glare she shot the interloper made him smile. The guy didn't have a chance.

What would Patthar have done? He'd turn on his charm and rescue the damsel in distress. Since this whole evening had been in Pat's honor, how could he do any less?

Of course, Pat would have gone for the busty, blonde friend. But something about this woman—tall and slender without being fashionably starved, a sense of quiet confidence, movements full of economy and a lethal grace—tugged at Akshay's attention.

He wound his way through the crowd, the alcohol buzz making him feel like he was floating. He'd been trying to drown the guilt rotting his gut with beer, but it hadn't worked. The memories of Patthar's last moments kept rolling through his head like a monsoon storm. Maybe the brunette would distract him.

"Hi, darlin'." He slipped his arm around her shoulders and pulled her snug. She smelled of fresh, clean rain. He wanted to nuzzle her neck, nip at the soft scented skin. "Sorry to keep you waiting."

The cowboy gawked and the woman almost jumped off the barstool. Up close, the lean muscles of her arm looked a whole lot more formidable. He sent her a djinn-to-djinn telepathic message: *Please don't hit me. I'm a good guy…really.*

She relaxed in Akshay's arms, making him warm and hard all at the same time. He forced all expression off his face and stared head-on at the other man. "You hitting on my girl?"

"Hey, I didn't know she was with somebody." Pretty Face held up both hands. "I was just being social."

Akshay thrust himself between them and flexed his biceps in the guy's face. He was taller and larger than Pretty Face. "You're in my seat."

The man slid off the stool and disappeared into the crowd. Akshay grinned after him.

"You can let go now."

Her husky voice and matter-of-fact tone yanked him back to reality. He was holding onto a seriously sexy woman. The black tanktop and tight blue jeans revealed delicious curves, lean muscles and long legs. Her flesh burned hot under his fingers. Akshay released her super-fast and stepped back.

She folded her arms across her chest and tilted her chin up. "So, I have been waiting for you, huh?"

"All your life." Oh sheesh. Now she'd hit him.

"Oh really?" She quirked a brow at him. "Well, then I should at least know your name."

Relief flooded through him. Okay, so Pat's method actually worked...even for him. "Shay."

"Thanks for your help, Shay," she said, indicating the empty stool. "I'm Maya."

Something about her filled him with a haunting familiarity, like her face had been imprinted in his psyche. "Have we met before?"

She rolled her eyes. "Oh please, I think we are past those old pick up lines."

The band struck up an old favorite, "Amarillo by Morning," and saved him. "May I have this dance?"

"I guess I owe you one."

"Not really," he shrugged. "I think you could have taken him, but I'm glad I got the chance to meet you."

She smiled and hopped off the stool.

Akshay let her precede him to the dance floor. His gaze traveled up her long legs and fixed on the roll of her pert heart-shaped ass. Damn, those jeans looked good on her.

On the dance floor, they turned to each other. As natural as traveling between two dimensions, his hand rested at her waist and he drew her close. Every breath of air smelled sweet and crisp, washed away other thoughts.

She looked at him, smiled and slid her hands up his arms, around his neck. A thrill chased through him at her touch. Akshay stared into her beautiful whiskey-colored eyes, his heart beating too fast as if he stood at the brink of his life staring at tomorrow, at the beginning of something.

"What? Do I have something on my face?"

"No."

"Stop staring at me."

"I can't."

A slow blush rolled across her elfin features and her gaze dipped. She closed her eyes and rested her head on his left shoulder as they danced in slow circles around the room. Every nerve in his body came alive and aware of soft, warm skin, the tickle of silky hair, and her intoxicating, heady scent. He was lost, so lost. Lost in the music, the moment and in Maya.

Two sets of hands grabbed Akshay from behind and tore him away from the dance. Rage surged to dangerous levels as the fancy cowboy grabbed Maya's hand and jerked her toward him.

"No one makes a fool of Bo Harlan," the cowboy sneered.

The two men holding Akshay snickered. Then Harlan reared back and punched him in the face.

Akshay's head snapped back and he tasted blood. Maintaining human-guise had its drawbacks. He righted himself and stared at Harlan.

"Let her go," he said. Akshay took a calming breath, wrestling to tamp down his growing fury. He could feel the tremble deep in his core, ready to call to the earth to crack open and swallow, bring this whole damn place down. *Control yourself. Humans break easily.*

Another breath. The lightning-laced scent of a brewing storm inside the club startled him, held him frozen for a moment.

With a grunt, he heaved and smashed his two captors together, headfirst. They slipped to the floor and lay still.

Maya stomped on Harlan's foot and followed with an uppercut.

With a yell, the bull rider let go of her, but within moments he reared back, hand raised to strike.

Akshay lunged forward, but Hagen, the new captain of his guard, tackled Bo and knocked over a couple of tables in the process. And that set off a dynamite of a fight—the whole bar jumped into the brawl, arms and legs lashed out, chairs and pool cues smashed, bodies stumbled and shoved. Akshay fought his way through the crowd, searching for Maya.

A red-faced man threw a punch at him. Years of warrior training made Akshay jerk away from the hit and return with an uppercut that sent the man sprawling.

Someone grabbed his arm. Akshay swung around, ready to smash whomever into smithereens, and found Maya staring at him. His heart pounded as he lowered his hand. She pulled him down behind an overturned table. They sat next to each other, panting as they watched the fight for a moment.

He glanced over at her. "Are you okay?"

She nodded.

"So where are you from?"

She pinned him with her golden gaze, lifted her chin in challenge. "I'm not really interested in getting to know you, just your body."

He stiffened and held her gaze. How dare she treat him like a plaything? His body told him to shut the hell up and appreciate her honesty and other assets. Akshay looked away, forcing himself to relax.

"Are you okay with that?"

"I'll learn to live with it." He'd end up marrying some politically advantageous princess chosen by his parents...so why not have some fun with a woman he found intriguing?

After a moment, Maya leaned over. "Want to step out for some fresh air and quiet?"

His head told him he shouldn't walk away from the fight, shouldn't abandon his guards. His rage wanted him to find Bo Harlan and pulverize him for touching Maya. His mother's voice whispered she was the wrong kind of girl. But the rest of him liked Maya's idea a hell of a lot. "Yes."

Akshay glanced at the crowd. His men were holding their own as was the blonde, who at that very moment elbowed a fat man in the gut. "What about your friend?"

The blonde took a break to grin and flash a thumbs-up before returning to pummeling someone else. Maya laughed. "Believe me, she'll be fine."

Shielding her with his body, Akshay grabbed Maya's hand in his and eased toward the door. They stayed close to the wall and crept their way through the crowd. Dodging flying objects and bodies, they pushed through the door into the cool night air.

"Whew! It was hot in there." She twisted her long hair into a knot. Her sharp profile, covered by a thin sheen of sweat, glowed in the moonlight.

"Hot and crazy." Even sweaty and messy, the woman looked good. He wanted to kiss his way down the curve of her cheek, along the length of her throat, into the valley between her breasts and lower.

"Stop it!"

"What?"

Hands fisted at her hips, she glared. "You're staring again."

"Yes, I am." He stepped closer, brushed her face with the back of his hand. "You're beautiful."

"I thought I made it clear, no lines." Her voice was thick with a mix of emotion he couldn't quite grasp. He searched her face for clues.

She cupped his chin. "You're bleeding," she said. "Let's go back to your place and get you cleaned up."

He closed his eyes and concentrated on his essence, his mind working on healing and cleaning his outer appearance. After a moment, he opened his eyes. "All done."

She leaned into him, her breath a warm whisper on his skin. "Let's go back to your place anyway."

His head dipped toward her, drawn by the magnetic pull of her tempting scent. What he'd intended to be a quick stolen kiss, ignited a burning hunger. Her soft, full lips parted beneath his, and her tongue darted out playful, inviting. Heat sizzled to his groin and he deepened the kiss, his tongue chasing after hers into her sweet, hot mouth. Her hands slid up his back, fingers tangled in his hair.

Damn, he could find nirvana in her, with her. He groaned and wrapped her warm, soft body in his arms.

CHAPTER 3

Hot damn, the man was a good kisser. Maya stood swaying, glad for the powerful muscled arms enveloping her. Her heart raced, her head spun and her insides crackled and grew wet like melting ice. She closed her eyes and pulled in a deep breath. He smelled rich and spicy like dark soil and green forest, with deep intertwined shades of moss, peat, cedar and pine. One breath and calm descended on her. She opened her eyes and looked around.

Shay had transported them to a nice hotel bedroom with carefully chosen earth tones and impersonal details. Maya held onto him as she glanced at the large bed and tried to ignore the disappointment deep inside her. An anonymous hotel room was perfect for a one-night stand. So what the space held nothing more personal than his luggage?

He cleared his throat and nodded at the closed door. "Um, there's a living room," he said. "We can watch TV, talk."

"Less talk and more action." She pressed herself against him and reclaimed his mouth. No more stalling. A friendly roll in the hay, that's all this was. A sperm deposit.

The heat of their kiss melted her against the hard planes of his body, brought her to a quick simmer. The image of him, strong and dangerous like a human battle axe, as he cut his way through the bar fight flashed through her. His face savage and his eyes searching until they met hers...then his gaze had darkened with want. A whimper escaped her as she grew wet between her legs.

He slipped his hand under her tank. The rough caress of his calloused fingers on her sensitive skin made intense pleasure shiver through her. The rhythm of their breath changed, matched the urgency of their need. She broke from the kiss and lightly bit his chin, careful not to break skin. He tasted salty sweet.

She laid her palms flat on his wide chest and pushed him down onto the bed, then climbed on top. Her nipples tightened and tingled, her sex wept with need. "Clothes," she rasped. "Get rid of them."

"Condom?"

"Why? We don't have to worry about human disease." She placed another soft bite at his throat. "I'm full djinn, I won't get pregnant unless I will it."

They both vanished their clothes at the same time. He wasn't cover-model handsome, all scars, sharp angles and strong, hard lines. Yet, all of it combined together into a sexy and very male package. Tall and built, the man was solid muscle. Powerful. Her eyes lingered on his erection, fierce and beautiful.

Oh, she wanted him. She wanted to lick him, touch him, possess him. And she wanted to be possessed by him in return, she wanted his thick, dark shaft deep inside her. Oh damn, she needed him *now*.

He skimmed a finger over the puckered seam of the recent injury on her arm and she stiffened. Shay sported scars enough to dwarf her, yet a weight settled in her limbs. Men—even battle-scarred men—preferred pretty women with soft, unblemished skin.

"You have a lot of scars."

"Is that a problem?"

A faint smile touched his lips. "No, I think we are well matched." His lips parted as if he had more to say.

"No questions, no soft courtesies."

His body tensed. "What then?"

"You and me." She licked her lips. "Hard and fast."

Maya fell on him with a hunger she'd never felt before. Flashes of the battlefield flew through her mind, the armor-covered earth djinn slicing down at her, the reek of blood, almost dying. Tears threatened. Her need to have sex, create life, twisted tight in her gut.

His hands slid up her torso until they grasped her aching breasts, his thumbs rubbed across her tight nipples. Shivers rippled through Maya. A moan slid from the back of her throat.

She leaned down to kiss him, and one of his big, rough hands slid lower and cupped her mound, kneaded and rubbed. A warm tingle spread through her as their essences started roiling and heating, edges blurred and she could feel him melting into her. Both their bodies glowed like banked coals.

"No," she gasped. "Hold onto your human form. It feels good, so good."

"Your wish is my command," he whispered.

Shay grasped the back of her head and rolled them over so he ended up on top, staring down into her eyes.

This close, this turned on, his eyes were like melted dark chocolate, with wide black pupils and glowing flecks of gold and emerald framed by lush dark lashes.

"You are beautiful," he said. Then he thrust into her. His hard length filled her, stretched her insides. The muscles of her sex quivered and clenched. An involuntary "Oh" escaped her lips.

He pulled almost all the way out, and then did it all over again.

The slide and slap of sweat-dampened flesh, the full length of his erection gliding in and out of her, his mouth sucking on one breast, then the other, filled her with delicious friction. Breath and rhythm increased in tempo as their bodies moved together in an intimate dance. Maya closed her eyes as the warm glow of an orgasm built inside her and let out soft pants of breath. She clutched his muscled arms.

An almost painful tug on her hair made her eyes fly open.

"Look at me," he commanded, continuing to move. His gaze had grown darker, wilder, and she almost imagined shadows chasing shadows deep inside. Her body arched as the first wave of an orgasm blasted through her. She screamed. "Oh damn, ohhdamodam!"

Satisfaction blazed through Akshay as Maya arched and screamed beneath him. He gave his all—touching her, teasing her, tasting her. He dove into her again and again, desperate to outrun the chaos in his head, until both of them were trapped in a web of need.

He only regretted that her beautiful eyes, like living, breathing pools of molten gold, pools with hidden secret depths, had clenched shut at the last moment, hiding her naked soul from him. A breath eased out of him. That was okay. Next time.

He kept riding her soft, shuddering body. There would be a next time and more, he promised himself. He'd keep making love to her until he forgot his past, left behind his guilty memories, until she totally possessed him.

Heat and pleasure crackled through his essence, overwhelmed his thoughts. Almost, almost, almost. "Oh, Maya, I'm coming."

"Hold on," she gasped. "Hold on to your form."

What was her fucking obsession with human forms? Both their skins glowed, light trying to burst through the unnatural barrier of human skin. But damn, she wanted him as a man. He gritted his teeth and held on to his form. Then he slammed into her one last time and cried out her name, drowning out her screams.

Akshay collapsed on top of her, still buried in her. He closed his eyes against the spinning room. Wow. Soft shudders shot through their bodies as the sound of their ragged breathing filled the air. He held Maya as their heartbeats slowed, their essences settled and their skins lost the ethereal glow. After a long moment, when he could think again, he swallowed to moisten his mouth. He nuzzled her ear, drinking deep of her rain scent, and whispered, "I want to make love to you as djinns do."

She shifted in his arms and answered with a soft snore.

Years of waking up early for weapons training kicked in and Maya woke in a room dimly lit by early morning light filtering in from the window. Her gaze landed on Shay's face framed by tousled dark hair.

Damn, he was beautiful. Sleep softened the hardness of his features, removed the closed off, wary look he wore last night, made him look younger. A soft smile tugged at his lips. She wanted to kiss him at the corner of his mouth, wake him with kisses, make love to him again...taking all the time and care in the world.

But it was time to leave. The deed was done. She'd felt the spill of his essence flood her in a hot rush, sensed his seed streaming through her, knew the exact moment when one had embedded itself in an egg hidden deep inside. A female djinn knew her body down to the most basic cellular level. She should slip out of the bed, out of the room, and out of his life.

Instead, some obscure need kept her anchored. She lay there watching the rise and fall of his chest, listening to the steady rhythm of his heart, breathing in his heady scent of sunshine and sweat.

A sudden chill invaded the room, made her stiffen. Goose bumps ran rampant over her skin and tension pebbled inside. Had the air-conditioner kicked on? She hadn't heard any telltale hum of machinery. The air just beyond Shay flickered and vibrated, sending a warning sliding through her essence. She lay still, eyes half-closed and pretending to be asleep. Within a breath or two, tendrils of smoke coalesced into a dark, hooded shape. An assassin born of air and soft, shifting shadows. Shit. She was buck naked and without a weapon. A silver dagger glinted in the glare of daylight and swooped toward Shay.

Without thinking, she pulled in a deep breath, gathering up all the magic from within and around her, focusing hard to think it into solidity and create a tangible barrier. As she repeated the words of the spell in her head, the air heated and boiled, turned malleable then hard. She pushed this shield of magic at the shadow foe. The blade hit the invisible protection with a loud thunk.

The assassin attacked again, and again, moving in a whirl of shadow and steel. She clenched her jaw and moved the magic around to match his speed and block his strikes. Movement behind her and a muttered oath alerted her Shay was awake. The attacks grew wilder, more frenzied. She concentrated on the assassin and her magic. Even a moment's distraction was dangerous.

"Get out of the way, Maya!"

Shay gripped her left shoulder, breaking her concentration. The shield snapped and all that accumulated magic crashed down on her like a fucking landslide. Her body crumpled and the blade plunged inside her human flesh. Swallowing her gasp of pain, Maya fought hard to hold onto her human shape as darkness descended.

CHAPTER 4

Maya awakened to harsh voices arguing and a room hot and oppressive with anger. A slash of pain burned her left side, while the rest of her felt like a squeezed-out sponge. Pain throbbed at her temples. She lay still and pretended to be out. Irritation flared, she seemed to be playing possum a lot lately.

"Son, you are the crown prince," said a gravelly male voice, weighed down by weariness. "Your duty is to be in the council chambers."

Crown Prince?

"I have told them everything I know," Shay's deep, dark tones answered. "The water djinns sent an assassin. We fought him off."

What? Panic spiraled in her gut making her nauseous. She imagined calming light filling her and cleared the jitters from her mind, forced her body to stay relaxed and limp.

"But you should be there to help strategize," frustration sharpened the man's reply. "And there're other state matters you need to learn about, be part of.

You need to be beside me, doing your duty. That's what protocol demands."

Strategize? Strategize about what? Dread made her bones heavy as stones.

"And what of honor and debt?" Shay's voice held an edge. "What does protocol say about those? This woman saved my life. I owe her."

A muffled curse she couldn't quite catch.

"We appreciate what she's done, but she should be in the healing center." A calmer, firmer female voice now. "Keeping her in your room doesn't make sense."

"The healer comes here and she is getting the care she needs." Was that a defensive quaver in Shay's tone? Maya wished she could risk a peek at his face, at all the faces in the room. But she quelled her curiosity.

A sigh that spoke volumes about disappointment filled the silence. "You're the crown prince, and single," the woman said. "And this girl—we don't know who she is, what family she is from, or what kind of djinn she is…all we know of her is this unimpressive human form, her willingness to bed you, and the name Maya. Your attachment is unseemly."

A rough scrape of a chair being pushed back. "Mother." Anger heated Shay's voice. "I guess you should go offer prayers that at least I'm not betrothed and shacking up with the unsuitable woman who saved my life."

"Akshay —"

"Please leave before either of us says things we'll both regret."

A rustle of cloth, the march of footsteps, and then the door closed smartly, just shy of a slam.

Another sigh, a release of tension. "You can stop pretending," Shay said. "I know you're conscious."

She looked up into his serious face. Concern warmed his eyes, sparked an answering warmth somewhere deep inside, in the vicinity of her heart. She noted the tired bags under his eyes, the raked-through hair that stood up in all directions. Throughout the night she'd woken up to find him sitting by her bed, stroking her hair, urging her to get well. And kisses—kisses on her forehead, kisses on her lips. Perhaps she'd dreamed the kisses.

"How?" Her voice was scratchy and raw. "How did you know?"

"Your breathing changed." He looked away. "I'm sorry you had to hear all that."

She looked around. She lay in a room with stone walls—beautiful white stones that shimmered with veins of rich rust and ochre—and dark wood finishes on the windows, rafters, fireplace mantle. A large iron shield with a sheaf of wheat at its center and swords hung on the far wall. A row of books lined the mantle.

"Where am I?"

"In my room."

Heat flushed through Maya as she realized she was also in his bed. A large, comfy sleigh bed, also fashioned out of dark wood and polished to a warm shine. Naked and wrapped in his sheets—deep gold, silky soft sateen sheets. Her throat dried and her voice cracked.

"I got that," she said. "What part of the universe is your room in?"

"The part you didn't care to know about." He smirked at her.

She so didn't have time for games. Unease gnawed in her gut. "Could you just, please, tell me where I am?"

"Bhramadesh."

Oh damn. The land of the earth djinns. Yup, that would explain his sexy sunshine scent.

"Crown prince?" she whispered.

"Prince Akshay Dar Zammen at your service." He clicked his heels and gave her short, stiff bow.

Oh double damn. Oh shit. She was pregnant with a royal earth djinn's baby.

The enemy's baby.

Her gorge rose in a bitter wave. She swallowed it down. How crazy-assed ridiculous could life get? She shot up straight in bed, not caring that the covers fell away, ignoring the stitch of pain that shot through her side. "Why the hell didn't you introduce yourself like this when we met?"

He slumped into the chair at her bedside and played with the bronze bracelet on his right wrist. "You really didn't seem to care."

His face darkened as he stared at his large, calloused hands. Hands that had caressed and stroked their way up her spine, made her moan. "Besides, I wanted to be Shay, just plain Shay," he said in a low voice. "I wanted to forget the duties and the costs that come with the crown."

An unfamiliar softening, again in the vicinity of her heart, startled Maya. She wanted to grab him by his hair and pull him in close, kiss away the worry and sadness in his face. No, no, no…he was the enemy. He didn't act like one though. She shook her head to clear it. "Why did you bring me to your home of all places?"

His head shot up and his lips tightened. "You were hurt," he said. "I didn't know where else to take you."

Panic churned anger inside her, denied the logic of his words. "I wouldn't have been hurt, if not for your interference!"

He rose out of his chair and towered over her. "You wouldn't have been hurt if you'd done the sensible thing and let *me* handle it."

"Oh!" Her hands curled into fists. "Next time, I'll just let you get stabbed."

He leaned close, just inches from her. "I'd prefer that to having you bleeding to death in my arms."

Akshay's hands gripped her shoulders and he locked down on her mouth with his. He bit her lips, pushed his tongue into her mouth, claimed her with a bruising, punishing kiss. Maya stiffened in his arms, until the heat from the kiss suffused her cells, made her lean into him, forget everything. The anger dissipated, leaving behind a slow, sexy exploration of tongues and teeth.

His hands shifted, sliding up and down her back, pulling her closer. Her breasts pushed against his chest, the rough scratch of his shirt on her peaked nipples set her trembling. His hand slid over her skin, making its way to the front, and touched the bandage.

She hissed in pain and he froze. He broke the kiss and rested his head against hers. "Sorry, I'm so sorry," he whispered. "You're hurt and I'm acting like a brute."

He laid Maya gently back down on the pillow and covered her with the sheet. "Tell me where you are from, and I'll take you there."

Oh shit. Her gut quivered. The kiss, the entire situation, had shaken her to the core and she scrambled to order her thoughts. Damn, she needed an excuse he'd buy.

"Uh, can you imagine my father's face if you walk in with me?" Not to mention, her mother's and Denidra's reactions. She shuddered at the mental picture that popped up. "I don't want my family to know what I was up to last night."

He blushed and ducked his head.

"If you just drop me off at the crossroads of the djinn and human dimensions, I can make my way back home."

"You wouldn't get far in your weakened state." He looked at her, a frown creasing his brow. "You know if you'd just revert to your djinn form, you'd heal faster."

"I-I can't." Panic drummed through her essence.

"Why not?"

Again with the questions. "I-I'm half-human," she whispered. "I can't change forms."

His jaw clenched. "You told me you were full djinn," he said, his voice dark and dangerous. "And what the hell were you doing during the fight? I have never seen magic like that."

"I was trying to protect us both with whatever little power I do have." Damn it, she couldn't tell him about her witch magic. She shrugged and opted for a half-truth. "I don't know. Maybe it comes from my human side."

"Why did you lie to me?"

Maya pulled the covers up to her chin. She didn't want to do magic because that would weaken her further, give her away if she pulled on the easiest power—water energy. Too bad she couldn't wish weapons into existence like clothes. She might need them if she had to fight her way out of this mess.

"Answer me."

"Because you full djinns look down on us half-breeds," she glared at him. Anger sizzled and burned inside her, anger at being cornered and forced to lie. "Just drop me off."

He folded his arms across his impressive chest and narrowed his eyes at her. "Either I'm carrying you back home." His gaze glittered cold and hard. "Or you can recover and talk to me again. Next time, ask nice."

He swerved on his heels and stomped from the room, slamming the door behind him.

Damn infuriating sexy man!

Now that she was awake and alone, Maya lay in bed and cleared her mind. She wished herself into a soft cotton shift dress of deep blue, reminiscent of ocean waters, and then contacted Denidra. Her aunt would be the calmer choice, and she'd pass the message on to her mother. Still she'd have to be careful and not create useless panic. She'd try to get out of this predicament without causing another war.

Finally! I was about to send out a search party. Are you okay?

Still alive and kicking.

I'm hoping you forgot the time because you're busy in bed.

She rolled her eyes. *Well, I am in bed.*

Denidra chuckled. *Good. When can we expect you?*

I'm going to take a few days.

Oooh, that good, huh?

No comment.

Laughter echoed in Maya's head. *Okay, let me know if you need anything.*

Maya clenched the bed sheet in her fists as the connection faded to nothing. She wished Denidra could fly in and rescue her. Not happening.

A flutter of wings drew her attention to the window. A gray-brown mourning dove settled on the ledge, bobbing its head this way and that, checking her out. It uttered a drawn-out call like a soft lament. Maya held still, not wanting to frighten the beautiful creature away.

The bird flew into the room and perched on the chair next to the bed, settling its black-smudged wing tips close to its body. Within seconds it dissolved into smoke, and Maya's internal warning pinged belatedly. She scooted back as far as she could, and looked around for a weapon. Her gaze landed on the bedside lamp. She grabbed it and held it like a bat.

The smoke thickened into a sleek silver gray female form, then details emerged and knitted together into a beautiful woman as pale and slender as the new moon, dressed in a soft shimmering gray gown, simple and elegant in its cut. She stared at Maya with somber kohl-lined gray eyes. "So you are Prince Akshay's woman."

Maya bristled. "No, I'm *not* Prince Akshay's woman."

The woman's eyes widened. "But you're the woman he brought in last night, naked, the woman the whole court is talking about."

Oh hell. Maya sighed. "I suppose…and you are?"

"I'm Umber, the king's second wife." An amused smiled flickered on the woman's lips as she eyed the makeshift weapon. "I'm not here to harm you."

Maya lowered the lamp, but still held onto it. Umber looked about Denidra's age, but more fragile. "Why are you here?"

"I was curious," she said. "But I should offer you my congratulations!"

"What for?"

"For the son you're carrying." Her bright smile faltered as Maya made choking sounds. "Are you okay? Let me call the healer."

"No," Maya gasped out. She swallowed a few times. "What makes you think I'm pregnant?"

Umber blushed prettily and cast a quick glance at the closed door. "My people are from the Northern deserts at the edge of this land," she said in a low voice. Her color deepened. "I have some human-magic in my blood line. Nothing fancy, but I can look at a woman and tell if she's pregnant, determine the baby's sex and health, time of birth...small things."

"Huh, useful." A faintness enveloped Maya and she slumped down on her pillow, letting the lamp fall to her side. Where djinn magic created illusions and allowed users to work elements they had a natural affinity for, human magic—when strong—allowed the user to manipulate others. Had the woman also sensed her water djinn nature? She didn't seem to be acting like it. "Who else knows?"

"The healer, of course."

"Damn, damn, damn!" Maya clenched her eyes shut, but hot tears still squeezed out.

"Don't worry, Akshay will marry you." Umber's hand patted her shoulder. "His father married me when I became pregnant. They take care of what is theirs."

Spend a lifetime among the male chauvinist earth djinn? Raise her child in an alien society, far from the family she loved? "I don't want to marry him!" she wailed, breaking into body-wracking sobs.

Umber murmured something in a dialect not familiar to Maya and enveloped her in a warm hug. Maya buried her face into the queen's shoulder and breathed in her delicate jasmine scent. The soft, soothing lilt of Umber's crooning flowed over her like warm water.

"Did you come...willingly?"

Maya hesitated and then answered. "I was unconscious."

Umber leaned her head against hers. "I...I was brought here fully conscious and terrified."

"Brought here?"

"My clan people are merchants and the king came across our caravan, saw me, and decided to have me," she said. "He gave my father a bag of gold."

"Your father sold you?" A wave of dizziness washed over Maya and the bedroom swayed.

"Our clan was no match for the king's soldiers. The bag of gold was mere courtesy, but enough to feed the clan for two winters." The queen released her and stood. She smoothed her dress down, fussing at imaginary wrinkles. "What the king wants, he gets. That is the way of powerful men."

Cold despair flooded Maya's thoughts, threatened to drown her. "Please help me," she said. "You have to help me escape."

Harsh, hollow laughter—if it could be called that—rang out. "Escape? I don't think it's possible, especially now that you carry a son. I spent most of my life searching for a way out."

Maya stared at Umber, noticed that haunted look trapped in her eyes, the sunken cheeks, the downturned corners of her mouth. The woman had given up and embraced her bitter fate. Maya wouldn't. As long as there was life in her, she wouldn't.

"Then please keep my condition a secret." She grabbed the queen's hand. "Please ask the healer to keep my secret...until I can figure a way out."

The queen gave her a pitying look and squeezed her hand. "As you wish."

With a soft sighing whisper, Umber's corporeal form dissolved into swirling dust and then reformed into the mourning dove. With a sorrowful cry and a flutter of wings, she flew out of the window into the endless blue sky.

CHAPTER 5

Sequestered in the council chambers with the inner circle, Akshay should have been thinking about war and strategy. Instead his mind kept drifting to thoughts of Maya, who now lay in his bed.

Naked, beautiful Maya. Pert breasts capped by dark chocolate nipples, lush sweet hips, long strong legs parted to reveal the glistening pink flower at her center, peeking out from a thatch of black curls. A twinge of sexual need zapped him, left him hard in a room full of men. Akshay slid lower in his seat, grateful for the large table hiding him. His left hand drifted over to the erection tenting his pants. Each stroke of his thumb against the solid ridge sent delicious shivers through him.

"We should attack!" Councilman Heggi banged on the table.

"We tried that recently," was the silky soft reply from Jazzaz.

"Maybe this time the outcome would be different." The councilman's face purpled, his essence pulsing bright under the human appearance he'd assumed. "The Water Djinns use of assassins in battle is most devious, dishonorable. Protocol says—"

Akshay tuned out the lecture on protocol and returned to more pleasant thoughts.

Strong and leanly muscled, her skin tattooed by scars, Maya was nothing like the fussy, swooning women his mother wanted him to meet. He liked his sex hard and rough, unrestrained and primal, and those women were too fragile…but not Maya. One tantalizing taste of her, the way she'd claimed him, gave him hope. She'd be his equal.

An angry banging on the table jolted Akshay to attention.

"I say we send an official complaint to the City of Brass and ask the Emperor of all Djinns to intervene. Creator knows we pay enough in tributes," Councilman Heggi's heated voice was almost a shout. "The water djinns must be punished."

"Are we sure the assassins were sent by the water djinns?" Councilman Achmed asked. His voice, measured and soft, tread carefully into the conversation.

"Of course," Akshay said, raking his hand through his hair. The dark specter of the assassin rose in his mind, fluttered there. He'd stopped dreaming of them since Maya. "The first ones attacked me on the battlefield. They hoped to take me when I was busy fighting. But—"

He cleared the dampness clogging his throat. "Patthar saved me."

Nods greeted his words. Akshay steepled his fingers on his chest. "What I can't figure out is why attack me?"

Jazz looked up from the map of the djinn world spread on the table. "You are the Crown Prince."

"Now, yes. But I wasn't then."

"Ah, but they knew you were our strength," King Zammen said. "They know I am old and ready to step down."

"And I do have a reputation of a frivolous fancy pants," Jazzaz interjected. "Good for a party, but not much else."

"They'd be fools to believe that façade," Akshay muttered, earning a smile from his brother.

"True, whoever sent the assassins must be a fool as well as a coward," the king said. "They figured with you dead, the leadership would be left to an old man and a dandy, and we'd be weak and easy to defeat."

More nods around the table.

"What's confounding me is that they got the desert rhakshas to switch alliances," Akshay said. "I couldn't believe it when they popped up in battle."

Heggi sneered. "Those barbarians can be bought and sold."

Jazz leaned back in his chair, fixing a steel-cold stare on Heggi. "Have some care with your words Councilor. You speak of my mother's people."

"Oh, no, no offense meant Sire. None at all," Heggi bobbed in his chair. "Once a woman marries, she belongs to her husband's tribe."

"We have more important things to discuss than women's lineages," the king interjected. "We will send an envoy to the desert folks to see where things stand."

He turned to Akshay. "Furthermore, the woman you have brought home—"

"Maya."

The king cut him a glare, and then continued. "She could very well be a plant from the same people. A spy."

"She could be a water djinn for all we know!" Heggi worried his collar.

Akshay grasped the edge of the table, his knuckles turned white as he leaned forward. "We have had this discussion," he bit out. "She saved my life."

"True." Jazz inclined his head. "What better way to ingratiate herself to you?"

"Enough!" Akshay shoved his chair back and stood. She couldn't be the enemy, couldn't be part of those who'd murdered his friend.

His father mirrored him. "Stop thinking like a man, and think like a king!"

"And what would a king do?"

"I would definitely not put her in my bedroom." King Zammen released a long sigh and rubbed the bridge of his nose. "The safer, more sensible, thing would be to put her in the dungeon and interrogate her."

"That would be a very fine thank you." The icy hands of dread wrapped around Akshay's heart. The woman certainly had secrets, yet the very thought of her being interrogated left him cold with fear. Maya, his Maya, thrown into a dark, dingy cell, manacled and behind bars. At the mercy of an interrogator, a man who specialized in pain and twisting the truth out of djinn souls. A man who broke full-blood djinns. Never.

Ignoring the panic knotting his guts, Akshay straightened and cast a cold look around the room. "No one touches her but me."

Silence greeted his words.

"That would work," Jazz leaned back in his chair. "I have always preferred interrogation through seduction."

"I shall do my duty." Akshay managed a stiff bow and stalked out of the room.

If only she could find a running source of water, she'd be replenished. Her essence would suck the energy from it until cool, refreshing power rushed through her veins again. Maya stared around the bathroom, despair pooling in her gut. The gray stone room was stark. A stone bench with a hole served as the toilet. An iron cover lay on top. Thank the Creator, the toilet was set under an open window letting in fresh air.

Maya hurried over and lifted the cover, wrinkled her nose in distaste. Metal bars ran across the hole as they did across the window, which led to a steep drop. She slammed the cover shut. Relief shuddered through her. The toilet chute hadn't been her choice option. No running water, and no way to escape.

She scanned the rest of the room. A large granite tub sat in the center of the room. Next to it stood a large covered metal bucket with a long-handled mug. A table held bowls of clay, salt and soap, a brush and comb. The washbasin too had a chute to drain the dirty water. But instead of a faucet, a fat-bellied copper pot held water. A matching mug for pouring sat next to it. Primitive. Worse than primitive, useless for her needs. Tears burned her eyes.

"Maya!"

Her head jerked up at Shay's bellow. She swiped at her eyes and tramped to the bedroom, allowing the heavy wood doors to slam shut behind her. "What?"

He glared at her. "I didn't know where you were."

"Can I not even go to the privy without permission?"

"Of course." He blushed and his voice turned down a few notches. "How are you?"

"I'm going crazy stuck in here. I need fresh air, running water, anything to escape this trapped feeling."

"Your wish is my command."

"I—what?" She'd been prepared to argue, bully, beg...even turn on the waterworks if needed. Wariness settled in her bones. "You'll let me out?"

"Even better. I will give you a personal tour." Keeping his gaze locked on hers, Akshay bowed to her. When he straightened, he snapped his fingers. A red and gold Persian carpet floated into existence and hovered next to them at mid-thigh height.

"We are riding on a Magic Carpet?"

"Yes."

"Isn't this a bit too Disney?" she asked, changing the dress into more practical clothes—jeans and a loose shirt. "The other djinns will laugh at us."

"I don't care. That was the best part of Aladdin." He grinned at her. She sucked in a breath at the flash of brilliance that transformed him from attractive to smoking hot sexy. Aiyiyiee.

"Besides this is the easiest way to take you around in your weakened state," he said. "And I'll make us invisible." He held out a hand to her.

Maya's heart hit the accelerator. Her head urged her to run. Fast. Shay was dangerous. Not dangerous like a soldier armed to the teeth. That she could handle. Dangerous like a man who could seduce a woman with his warm sunshine scent and mischief-filled grin, rock hard abs and love for fairytales. She pulled in a deep, shuddering breath and let it out. Then she placed her hand in his. Warmth sparked at their touch and rolled through her essence as she climbed aboard the carpet.

He settled in at her back. Awareness scorched her through the thin shirts separating them. Too close. She leaned against the strong wall of his chest and let his heat wrap around her.

Akshay lowered his head to her ear and whispered, "Ready?"

No. The tickle of hot breath on her sensitive skin sent tingles shooting to her core. Yes. *Shit, shit, shit.* She nodded, not trusting herself to speak.

"Hold on." His arms went around her in a loose hug. She kept her hands tightly interlocked in her lap.

The carpet rolled up on both sides, pushing them closer together. Her breath came in ragged gasps. Beneath her, the carpet trembled with barely checked power then shot forward, out the window and into the still-bright evening sky.

A scream ripped out of her and she clutched his arms, which tightened and pulled her snug in his lap. His laughter, rich and carefree, rang into the air as the carpet rocketed on. She could happily float in the music of that laugh.

The rush of air against her face eased as the carpet slowed. The gentle rocking soothed Maya, made her imagine she was on a boat drifting down a river, over a wide expanse of blue-green water glistening in the sun. Water, precious water. Her parched throat ached.

"Open your eyes."

His voice pulled her back to reality, and she grew aware that the air on her skin was hot and dry. She was aware of his hard ridge pressing against her. Aware of another kind of heat devouring her in the most delicious way possible. *Stop it. Think of something, anything, else.* Her eyes flew open.

They floated over the strangest garden. Fairies danced among trees, deer nibbled at shrubs, pavilions with the most delicate lattice work and flowering vines, trees, and more trees of every shape and size—all carved out of stone or fashioned in metal, or a beautiful combination of the two.

"Wow, I have never seen a garden like this," she said. "It's beautiful."

"We make do with what we have."

He steered the carpet lower and through a tunnel of trees. Silver, gold, copper and bronze leaves—beaten flat, shaped and decorated with grooved veins—shivered and shimmered in the breeze. A soft metallic tinkling laughed them out of the tunnel and into open air again.

"Would you like a tour of the castle?"

"Maybe later," Maya said. Since all she knew about the earth djinns was from books or others, she wouldn't pass up the opportunity for a first-hand look. Plus it could be useful intelligence. "I'd like to see a bit of your country."

His muscles tensed around her. "As you wish."

They flew toward a thick stone wall at the edge of the garden. Maya pressed into Shay as the carpet went up and over. Below them lay a shabby maze of faded tents and dusty paths. The djinns that milled around were like smears of watery light, shriveled into slivers of what they should be, their movements slow and shuffling. A few emaciated dogs slunk between the narrow stalls. A sweltering quiet gripped the place, filled Maya with unease.

Why was the place so silent? The markets back home were bustling, raucous places. Hawkers shouted out bargains and deals, djinns haggled back and forth. Dogs and children ran wild. She loved going to the market because it pulsed with vibrant energy. Not here.

"I'd like to get off and walk around."

"Are you sure?" Strain weighed his voice down.

She turned to look at him. Askhay's eyes had turned obsidian and flat. His whole body strung tight. Feelings of anger, sadness and frustration peeled off him in waves.

An inexplicable urge to retract her request filled Maya. She wanted to return to the carefree playfulness of the earlier part of the journey. She wanted to kiss his worries away. "Yes."

CHAPTER 6

Without another word, Akshay maneuvered the carpet into an empty area behind some stalls, where the shopkeepers' rides were parked. Tethered molewyrms barely lifted their heads to acknowledge them. One hissed half-heartedly as they climbed off the carpet.

Maya shrank against Akshay.

"They won't hurt you," he said, rubbing one's snout. "They're gentle creatures unless riled up."

Right. She'd seen them in action on the battlefield. "The merchants use these?"

He nodded. "Molewyrms can travel far in the desert without water and they can carry a lot."

She eased her shoulders and glanced back. So the destructive creatures actually had some use. "I'd like to continue invisible."

"Okay, though there's really not much to see," said Akshay, rolling up the carpet. He tucked it under one arm, and offered the other to her. She placed her hands at the crook of his arm and they walked on toward the market.

A few stalls displayed colorful strings of sliced dried fruit. Others sold dry goods with small hills of ground spices and milled flour, dried herbs. She pulled in greedy breaths as she passed these, enjoying the aroma.

Then came the crafts stalls. Potters squatted in the dirt, next to their earthen wares. Some were simple and utilitarian, made of red clay. Others had flourishes and designs, the maker's signatures. Metal workers displayed glittering fat-bottomed vessels, set one on top of the next creating shiny columns, serving as mirrors for those passing by.

Some of the djinns wore human guise and even these looked weary. With pinched faces and hunched shoulders, shopkeepers and customers transacted business in almost complete silence. Maya almost drowned under the tangle of emotions swirling around her. Being a water djinn, her awareness was sharper and she felt every emotion. Despair, bitterness, resignation with lingering wisps of hope. She wanted to fan that hope until it grew bright and fierce and spread like flame. She wanted to make these djinns smile.

A female stared straight at them. Maya's breath hitched and she stilled from the inside out. Could the woman see them?

The woman's gaze shone with a feverish hunger as her tongue flicked across her dry, cracked lips. A deep tone of a gong rang through the air, galvanizing her into action. The female djinn turned and snatched up the pot she'd just paid for, and then—with an unexpected burst of speed—headed toward them.

Akshay grabbed Maya's arm and pulled her out of the way. The woman rushed past them, stirring up dust.

What in two dimensions was that about? Maya twisted around. Djinns from all over the market streamed toward a building guarded by soldiers dressed in brown, green and gold uniforms. The colors of the earth djinn royals.

The djinns, old and young—even children—carrying pots, shuffled into a line that snaked from the top stair of the building all the way into the heart of the market. Massive doors swung open and excited whispers buzzed through the crowd. Maya dragged Akshay to the front to see better.

She watched as djinn after djinn hurried forward and soldiers ladled water into their pots, handed them bags of grain and lentils, and small bags of fresh fruits and vegetables.

What's going on? she asked Akshay in mind speak.

Rationing? She turned and stared at him. *Why?*

He stared at the people standing in line. *So everyone has something to live on.*

The stark truth of his words sank deep inside her. She could see the earth djinns were starved, but why? She'd seen pictures of fields of gold and read about their opulent harvest festivals. Had they all been lies?

Prickles of unease needled through her, whispered warnings of being watched. Maya whipped around, heart pounding. She barely caught a flicker of shadow from the corner of her eye.

You okay?

She searched the crowd, but all eyes stayed focused on the soldiers. Maybe she'd imagined the movement. Maybe being surrounded by earth djinns had her jumping at nothing. Yet, she couldn't shake the feeling that someone continued to watch them. Maya shivered and he drew her closer.

She nodded.

They walked back behind the tents in silence. "Where to next?" he asked.

Maya looked into his face. This man, the crown prince of the earth djinns, the enemy, the man she'd been intimate with and whose child she carried, the man who'd taken care of her, loved this place, these djinns. She wanted to see Bhramadesh the way he saw it. "Show me what you will."

He held her gaze with his, and then nodded and unrolled the carpet. Within seconds, they were airborne.

Soon the castle loomed in front, luminous and ghostly white in the dying light. A beacon Akshay homed in on. They zoomed through the stone garden, deeper and deeper into its heart, and this time the trees tinkled as if laughing at a secret until the carpet smoothly slid along the length of a hidden marbled porch and stopped in front of a pair of glass doors set in a glass house. Maya gasped. The house seemed packed full of plants. Real ones.

Akshay vaulted off the carpet, helped her down, and then made the carpet disappear. He grabbed her hand and pulled her to the door, as excited as a little boy at an aquarium. At the door he held his hand under the security scanner and let the machine read his bracelet. With a soft ping, the door slid open.

"The air djinns have it so much easier," he said, pulling her into a moist warm jungle of exotic and varied plants. "They can just breeze into any place they want to go."

Maya looked around in wonder at the organized chaos of plants growing under, over and around each other. Blooms of many colors flourished everywhere. Of course, water djinns couldn't go through a door either, but they could melt and flow underneath it…when they weren't pregnant or weakened. "I'm sure it's frustrating when you're in a hurry."

He glanced at her as they rounded a corner. His eyes, full of sympathy, swept over her human form. "Of course, you understand."

Guilt knotted her stomach. She hated lying, and yet had no choice. "Of course."

He smiled and turned her around. Rows and rows of vegetables grew from suspended baskets and spiraling supports rising from the ground. From leafy greens to squat squash, dangling beans to clusters of ripe tomatoes. "This is where we grow the vegetables that the soldiers were handing out."

"Using earth technology." She looked around at the glass panes all around. "This is what they call a greenhouse."

"You know of it?" He plucked dead leaves off plants as they passed.

She nodded, pleased by the spark of interest lighting his face. "I toured some famous garden on earth once, and they had a greenhouse. Much smaller than this."

"The djinns are spoilt by their reliance on magic, of having everything too easy…and now our world is fading and failing," his voice grew sad. "The humans worked on science and technology, kept trying to strengthen their existence, and they have much to teach us."

"So you learned from them."

He nodded. "Yes, I convinced my father to send me and some of the other young djinns to colleges in the human dimension. In fact, we have a lab inside the palace where scientists are working on creating more drought-tolerant plants."

She clapped her hands in delight, pleased at his resourcefulness. "I love what you've done, what you're doing."

A dusky blush rolled across his sharp cheekbones. "I am the crown prince, it's my duty to take care of my people."

Umber's words about powerful men floated back to her. Rulers didn't have to do anything, and some chose to do nothing beyond what benefited them. She was glad Akshay was a better man. "That is good, more than good," she said. "If you bought more water from the water djinns…" Her words faded at his scowl.

"We have offered them all kinds of riches and alliances, but they refuse to sell us more." He looked around. "But we try to make the best use of what they do give us, and we use the rich molewyrm castings as fertilizer."

Why would her mother's emissaries not sell more water? It didn't make sense. Very little made sense about this entire situation…except for the quiet pride in his voice, the straightening of his shoulders as he surveyed the plants.

She swayed on her feet, drained of all energy by everything she'd seen and felt, by the chaos of her thoughts, by the lack of opportunity to escape. He caught her, held her up and against his hard length.

"Oh Maya, I'm sorry." Regret shone in his eyes. "I got so excited playing tour guide, I have kept you out longer than I should."

"Don't worry," she said, resting her head on his shoulders. "I'm not sorry. I'm grateful for everything you showed me."

He swept her up in his arms. "My pleasure, but it's still bedtime for you."

When they arrived back at the room, a tray with spoons and two bowls of yellow rice and lentil stew waited for them. Akshay must have ordered the kitchen to send it up at some point. Maya's stomach growled at the first whiff of the spiced aroma, rich with cinnamon and cardamom. Bits of colorful vegetables dotted the mix.

"Let's eat, and then there's more," he said setting her down in a chair.

"More?" She wasn't sure she could take anymore.

"Yes." His gaze met hers and slid away. A soft smile played on his lips as he settled into the second chair and grabbed the other bowl and a spoon. Stolen glances, full of heat and promise, collided and skittered away as they wolfed down the meal in silence. Now that she'd seen the man beyond the hot bod, beyond his being an earth djinn, her essence seemed to be more aware of him, of his every breath, every move.

Akshay finished before she did. He set the bowl down on the tray and leapt from his chair. "Stay here," he said. "I'll get things ready for more."

He'd already reached the bathroom doors, when the question popped out. "What do you mean by more?"

He threw a wicked glance over his shoulder. "Good things come to those who wait."

She stifled a groan as he disappeared. Earlier this evening she'd been primed and ready for another bout of sex with him. After all, Akshay was a damn sexy djinn. Her conscience whispered—*enemy djinn*. She ignored it. But right now, all she wanted was a bath and bed.

The sound of water hitting stone sent a shiver through her. Was the man preparing a bath for her?

Her pulse revved in hope. Oh bless his soul! She twisted her hair into a messy topknot.

Impatience gnawed at her, made her set aside her bowl and tip-toe to the bathroom door. She peeked in. A soft golden glow illuminated the cavernous room from tiny bits of smokeless djinn flames weaving through the air like fire flies. Akshay stood naked by the full tub, scattering something over the water. Warm light and dark shadows played over his firm buttocks and rippling muscles. Creator, he was beautiful.

"What is that?"

"Dried jasmine," he said.

"From your greenhouse?"

"No, whenever one of us goes to earth, we try to collect something—flowers, fruits, seeds—to bring back," he said. "These were from my last trip to India. I love the scent."

She stepped further into the room, didn't stop until she was next to him. Maya breathed in the delicate, sweet scent of the flowers as they steeped in the water. Mmmm.

He glanced at her. "You're still dressed."

"I can vanish the clothes."

"No, don't." The soft words were like a command and brought her next thought to an abrupt halt. Her breath lodged in her throat as his eyes turned dark with desire.

He unbuttoned her shirt, tackling each button with unhurried, sure fingers until the fabric gaped, exposing a strip of skin from her throat to her navel. Air kissed her skin, made sensitive by anticipation, and she shivered.

Eyes still locked on hers, he gently peeled back the shirt, rolled it down her arms and let it fall to the floor.

Being small breasted, she hadn't bothered with a bra. Even though he'd seen every naked inch of her, somehow after spending the whole day with him, shyness crept in. Her arms wanted to fly to her breasts and cover them. But something in his hot, dark gaze stopped her.

He crouched and his eyes were at her navel. He slipped his fingers between the waist of her jeans and skin, made her gasp at the contact. Soon that button yielded to him, too. He inched her zipper down slow and easy, then grasped the waistband and dragged her jeans and panties down to her ankles. Maya placed a hand on his shoulder and stepped out of them. She stood completely naked. A flush of warmth washed through her.

Akshay blew softly at her mons, his breath trickling through her curls, making her tremble. Then he rose and placed butterfly kisses on her belly button, up her torso, on each of her breasts, at the base of her throat, on her chin, her mouth, the tip of her nose, her eyelids and, finally, her forehead. He stepped back and let his gaze caress her from the top of her head to the tips of her toes and back up again. A long breath escaped him. "You're beautiful."

Where once she'd have protested, Maya stayed silent. She could hear the honest awe in his voice, see the worshipful admiration in his eyes, feel the desire in the hardness of his aroused sex brushing against her skin.

All of it stunned her, left her speechless and filled her with the confidence of a woman. She took a step forward, closed the gap between them. She slid her palms in a sensual caress up his six-pack, across his manly shoulders until her arms snaked around him.

One hand grasped his back, the other fisted in his hair. "Kiss me."

He did. A deep languorous kiss, where he drank her like a parched man. His tongue explored her mouth, played tag with her tongue. He sucked and bit at intervals, creating sparks of pain and pleasure, as his hands roamed over her bare skin, until trembles quaked through her and the muscles in her legs turned shaky. Oh Creator, he was devouring her and she had no intention of stopping him. She couldn't.

He broke the kiss and scooped her up in his arms. He cradled her against his heaving chest as he pulled in one ragged breath after another. Desire wrapped them together, stirring up a primal hunger deep inside, making Maya ache between her legs.

Akshay turned and carefully climbed into the tub, lowered himself gently until fragrant, hot water—just beyond scalding—enveloped both of them. The water lapped at her skin, washed away the dust she wore, soothed her frayed spirit.

She closed her eyes, inhaled a deep breath of the flowery scent, and sank deeper into the tub. Her head lolled back against his shoulder, and her limbs relaxed as the heat soaked into her bones. This was perfect. It didn't make sense, but somehow, someway, being here like this, with this earth djinn, was perfect.

Maya's bent legs rested against his, and he moved his hands back and forth across her knees in long, lazy strokes.

"May I wash your hair?"

"My hair?"

"There are some leaves tangled in it," he said. "From the greenhouse."

Not to mention tons of dust, maybe even an insect or two. Yikes. She'd have to rethink flying carpet travel. Maya cringed. "Um, yes please. Thanks."

She hugged her knees and rested her chin on them, shutting her eyes. Deft fingers unraveled her topknot, massaged her scalp and threaded through her hair. She bit her lower lip to keep from moaning.

Warm water poured on top of her head, trickled down her face and neck. Strong fingers lathered soap into her hair, paused to gently unknot tangles. More water rushed through, washing away the soap and the day's debris. Next she felt the steady strokes of a comb. Stroke after gentle stroke.

"You have beautiful hair."

"It's straight and boring."

The combing stopped. *No, please don't stop. Don't stop.*

"You really don't see yourself, do you?"

Shagaard had mirrors, and she glanced in them at passing. "What do you see?"

"A beautiful woman." Akshay wound her hair around one hand, pulled it to the side. He kissed her exposed nape. A soft sigh escaped her. "A woman with silky soft hair that shimmers blue black."

Another kiss, this time on the side of her neck. Then he let her hair slide free of his grasp. "It's like running my fingers through night in all her glory."

She turned around. Their eyes held in silent communication. She found herself caught naked in his warm, honest gaze. Found herself falling headlong. And she trembled.

"Turn around, I'll scrub your back." His voice, rough with need, scraped along her skin. She did as she was told. He lifted her wet, heavy hair and laid it over one shoulder.

"On your knees."

Again she complied.

He used a wet cloth, slippery with soap, to gently cleanse her skin. The subtle abrasion of the cloth as he moved it in circles on her skin set off tiny quakes through her system. He shifted closer, making the water slosh, and slipped his arms beneath hers. He cupped a breast with one hand and used the soapy cloth to cleanse and massage it, then the other. Taking time to squeeze and roll her nipples. She closed her eyes and concentrated on her tattered breathing.

Too soon, he moved onto the valley between, soaped her bosom and throat, and then slipped down to soap her torso.

"You need to stand," he whispered.

Just the thought of his talented fingers slipping and sliding among the sensitive folds between her legs almost caused Maya to have an orgasm. She wet her lips and turned around. "My turn."

He gave up the cloth, placed his hands on his thighs and waited. Even though he wasn't standing at attention, she could feel the tension radiating off of him.

As she massaged his shoulders he let out a soft groan. She worked her way lower, almost to the erection trapped between them.

"Enough." He fumbled in the now cool water and pulled the plug. The water drained with loud sucking noises.

"Where is it going?"

"It'll be filtered and purified and used in the farms," he said.

The water had almost disappeared and left him exposed. She grasped his turgid penis in her washcloth covered hand and began moving up and down. With a muffled curse, Akshay snatched the cloth from her with a growl. "My turn."

CHAPTER 7

Heaven and hell. The damn woman was pure torture, overriding his good intentions. He had wanted to take care of her, and instead now all he wanted was to bend her over and take her. Hard.

A flash of Maya swaying on her feet in the greenhouse careened through his thoughts. No. Even though she didn't seem tired now, he'd sensed the weariness that blanched her skin pale, had noticed her holding her hurt side. She didn't need slam-bam sex, she needed soothing and sleep. Akshay pulled in a deep calming breath, slowly let it out. *Control yourself. You're the crown prince, you have to have control.*

Her wet, naked body glistened in the golden glow as she stood in front of him with her legs slightly parted, tempting him to touch and explore. She tossed him a saucy smile as he stared mesmerized. Akshay swallowed. A little payback wouldn't be amiss.

He started at her toes, and massaged his way up her legs, stopping to lightly stroke his thumb back and forth in the sensitive area behind her knees. Maya cursed as her legs buckled and she grabbed his shoulders to steady herself. He chuckled.

"Enjoying yourself?"

"Immensely." He slid his hand up her thighs to the edge of the beautiful triangle. She sucked in a breath. "Revenge has never been sweeter."

He stroked the mouth of her vagina with washcloth covered fingers. She moaned and lifted a leg up, resting the foot on the edge of the tub. He let the cloth drop and his soapy fingers explore. His thumb teased her clitoris with small, circular motions.

Her hips moved, dancing with his fingers, responding to a primal rhythm. She gripped his hair and pulled his face against the side of her abdomen. He lightly bit her right above her pelvic bone, then soothed the skin with slow circles of his tongue.

Maya moaned and pressed against him until he could feel the shaking beneath her skin. He continued to toy with her clit, while sliding his finger in and out. Panting, she half-squatted and opened herself up further. He obliged by pushing two fingers into her hot, wet core.

Ragged sounds emerged from her throat, drove him to distraction. *Control. Hold your control.* Her face turned toward the ceiling, her hands clutched him as she undulated following his lead. Her breasts, perky and flushed, danced and brushed against the top of his head. *Creator, she was beautiful.*

With a long drawn-out cry, Maya dissolved into shudders. Her body jerked and stiffened, then went limp against him. He wrapped his arms around her and gently lowered her to sit, leaning on him. Tucked her head beneath his chin.

"How do you feel?"

Skin to skin, he could feel her pounding heart. She dragged in great gulps of air. "Boneless." After a moment, she managed another word. "Content."

He kissed the top of her head. "Good."

Akshay grabbed an ewer full of water and poured it over her head.

"Oh!" Wonder brightened her voice. "It feels like rain."

Maya woke the next morning cuddled against a warm male body, held inside possessive brawny arms. She smiled. Last night had been heaven.

Oh, the water. The long deep soak, the rush of water over her skin. While it hadn't been fresh running water, it still helped heal her wounds both physical and elemental.

Akshay had bathed her, toweled her dry and tucked her into bed. Her face heated as other, less innocent, images flooded her mind, as she remembered every touch on her body, on her skin and inside. A breath shivered out of her. Okay, so he'd done a whole lot more. Left her completely satisfied and relaxed. Then curled around her and held her until she fell asleep.

A different kind of warmth wound its way through her, deeper than sexual heat. The warmth of a hug, of knowing someone had taken care of her without demanding or expecting anything in return, without wanting to use her as a connection to her family. When she'd tried to return the favor, Akshay had been gentle but firm. He'd said, "No, tonight is yours. You need to rest."

When she'd protested, he'd shared a knowing smile. "There will be more nights."

Her smile bloomed into a grin. Why wait for night? She snuggled back into Askhay, wriggling her hips for emphasis.

He stirred and hardened against her, his grasp tightening. He growled against her neck. "Stop that."

She stilled. "Don't you want me?"

"More than you can fathom," he said. "But I have to be in my father's court in a bit. I dare not be late."

"Is there something special planned?"

"On Fridays, the court is opened up to the public. Any citizen with a concern can ask for help." His fingers traced her scars. "I need to be there."

"I understand," she said. "When will you be back?"

"I don't know," he said. "The court stays in session as long as there are petitioners."

"Oh."

"What's wrong?"

"After the wonderful day yesterday, the thought of staying here with nothing to do is unbearable." Her voice quivered. "I'm sorry, I sound so self-centered."

He squeezed her tight for a moment. "My mother always says living is staying involved in the life around you."

A thought glimmered in Maya's mind. She needed to learn more about the earth djinn women. Compare notes to see whether she'd been as misinformed about them as she'd been about the water situation. "What will the women be doing? May I go join them?"

He stilled. "My mother can be difficult."

"I'll be on my best behavior."

He laughed and it rippled over her all warm and sexy, made desire stir inside again. "I seriously doubt if your definition of best behavior matches up with my mother's." He rose naked from the bed.

"Are you going to bathe?" Maya waggled her eyebrows. "Shall I wash your back?"

"No, that would mean a definite delay," he said. "Besides, I used up my quota of two-day's worth of water yesterday."

He wished some clothes on. "However, yes I think you should go hang out with the women of my family."

She dressed as well. "Why?"

He turned dark, serious eyes on her. "I want them to get to know you, care for you as I do."

With that simple sentence, he stole her breath and set her heart fluttering.

CHAPTER 8

Maya followed a female djinn servant through a labyrinth of cool corridors, until they finally approached a set of gold doors decorated with flowering vines created from vibrant jewels. She recalled her lessons—part of Shagaard's "know-your-enemies" policy—and mentally identified emeralds, peridot, rubies, sapphires, garnets, topaz, and more.

The irony of all that rich beauty twisted Maya's insides. All the diamonds of the world couldn't be turned into water, if the water djinns refused to sell. But why wasn't her mother allowing the sale? While the treasury wasn't completely empty, some of these jewels would definitely be useful in the coffers.

After a soft knock, the servant pulled open one of the doors and gestured Maya inside. Four sets of eyes—cool and assessing—fixed on her. She almost jumped out of her human skin as the door clicked shut.

Four women dressed in rich brocade and silks sat pressed close to the jali-screened marble partition—the latticed stonework as intricate as fine lace—that separated the men's world from the women's. Umber, her face devoid of any expression, was the first to turn away. Her lady-in-waiting—dressed the simplest in a moss-green silk with embossed gold daisies— took that as a cue and turned away as well. Maya got the hint and stopped herself from rushing to Umber's side. Instead, she bowed hastily to the older, hard-faced woman, dressed slightly richer than the rest. Queen Number One. Akshay's mother.

The queen acknowledged Maya with a stiff nod and returned her attention to beyond the screen. A young woman, who sported a similar plain oval face as the queen, but with more sweetness and softness, smiled shyly at her. Akshay's sister. Maya returned the smile and settled herself on a cushion equidistant from each queen.

Court was well in session, dealing with a dispute about a fruit tree. It was on one djinn's land, but grew over the fence of another. The petitioner complained that the neighbor was stealing fruit, while the neighbor argued he'd done no wrong since he took only what hung over his property.

The king's voice—which Maya recognized from when she'd first regained consciousness—grew harsher as he tried to convince one party to a payment plan, and then get both to agree to barter. But neither djinns refused to let go of their pride.

Akshay's sister whispered something to her mother. The queen smiled and picked up a coiled copper tube that ran from the room to the outside, and tapped on it twice. She waited until silence descended in court, and then spoke into it.

After a few minutes, the king spoke. "Since you have refused our counsel, hear our judgment," he said.

"Tomorrow at noon, the tree in question shall be chopped down by a royal gardener and all fruits will be collected and added to the royal ration for the greater good."

A moment of silence followed, and then came an anguished wail. Like the other women, Maya found herself pressing her face to the cold screen. She peered out of tiny gaps in the lattice.

The djinn in question shivered and flung himself to the floor. "Please don't cut down the tree, your Majesty, true son of Mother Earth," he said. "I have often ignored my own thirst to have water for the tree. I have taken care of it for years and it's a good, fruitful tree."

The king raised his hand and silenced him. Then he turned his head to other djinn, who looked equally miserable. "What say you?"

Maya wished she could see the king's face, but at least she had a good view of the petitioners. The other djinn stumbled forward. "The tree has helped feed my family for years, your Majesty," he said. "I, too, would beg you not to cut the tree."

"I agree it's a good tree," the king said. "But it has come between two neighbors, djinns who should be helping each other instead of attacking one another. I cannot allow that to continue. Have either of you any suggestions?"

The two djinns huddled together for a whispered conference. Then the neighbor djinn stepped forward. "Since Hashim planted the tree, watered and cared for it, since water is as precious as life, and I have enjoyed the fruit, it's only fair that I contribute one-third of all the water needed to help take care of the tree."

"Do you agree?"

The owner's head bobbed. "That is acceptable. I can use some of the water saved to grow something else perhaps," he said. "And Sadek can have all of the fruit that grows over his property."

"So be it." The king rose from the throne.

A scribe scribbled notes furiously as another official looking djinn banged a gavel on a table and cried, "The court is breaking for lunch!"

In the women's room, the princess and Maya stood back as the elder queen, Umber and her companion paraded out.

The princess flashed an impish smile. "Hi, I'm Ara, and you must be Akshay's mystery woman."

She shook her head and shared a rueful smile. "Yes, I guess I am, but please call me Maya."

Ara laughed and snagged Maya's arm with hers. "Come on, I'll take you to lunch."

"That's very kind of you."

"It's the least I can do," the girl shared. "For making my grumpy older brother a little less grumpy."

Her words sent a flush of pleasure through Maya, warming her in the deepest part of her heart. *Stop, don't smile so wide. You will give your feelings away.* "Well, I'm glad I have been of some use while your family gives me care and shelter."

Ara bent her head close. "So tell me all about you. Are you a water djinn spy?"

Maya tripped over her own foot. A hand reached out from her other side and steadied her. A tall, elegant man emerged from the shadows. She found herself staring into a handsome face with eyes as gray and cold as the winter sky. The man released her arm and gave her an elaborate bow. "Prince Jazzaz at your service."

"Thank you." She couldn't help staring at the man. Dressed in a silver-embroidered blue long coat, he was almost pretty. So unlike Akshay, but he had to be his half-brother. Another illusion crumbled. She'd expected Umber's son to be a boy, not a man. Certainly not a dangerous man.

"But please don't let me interrupt your conversation," he said. "So, are you a water djinn spy?"

"Oh Jazz, stop teasing," Ara scolded. "I was just joking with her."

"Unfortunately sister, I'm most seriously interested in her answer." He moved with languid grace to block their way. A smile twisted his lips, but didn't reach his eyes. "So are you a spy? Or a seductive siren trying to sleep your way into royalty?"

Maya's skin flashed hot, and then icy cold. Her mouth grew dry as she tried to form a response.

The man reached out and traced his fingertips down the side of her face and throat to the top of her silk-covered bosom.

She flinched and stepped back, arms rigid at her side to keep from pummeling him. Damn, she hated being helpless…and diplomatic.

His smile grew wider and he opened his mouth to speak. But before a single word could come out, a punch sent him stumbling back. Maya jerked into Ara.

A furious Akshay stood there, veins bulging in his thick neck, wide chest heaving, and murder in his eyes. "How dare you?"

Jazzaz pulled out a handkerchief from his breast pocket and pressed it to his bleeding lip. He stepped into Akshay's space. "I only said what everyone is thinking."

"Groundless stupidity doesn't need to be repeated."

"Is it groundless?" Jazzaz bit out. "Do you really know otherwise?"

Akshay stood silent as a stone statue.

"Yet, you bring her into your bedroom, give her a personal tour of our land, and allow her to listen into our court business." He paced with a lethal grace. "Unlike you, the rest of us aren't thinking with our dicks."

Maya had enough. "Stop it. Both of you," she said. "I promise you I mean you no harm, and it's clear I have over-pressed your hospitality. I will leave."

Akshay's angry gaze whipped to her. "You will do no such thing."

She turned to Ara. "I don't feel well, and would like to return to my—the room. Please."

"Of course." Ara hurried her past the two glaring men and down the corridor. The sound of scuffling and muffled oaths chased them on their way.

CHAPTER 9

Maya held onto her tattered control as they wound past others casting curious glances at her. Jazzaz's ugly words, his rude touch, haunted her. Did the rest truly think the same of her?

When they reached Akshay's room, Maya's body convulsed with strangled sobs. Ara shut the door and hugged her. "Let it out, just have a good cry."

"I-I don't want to cry," she managed at last. She rushed to the bathroom and picked up the water pot next to the sink and drank from it. The cool rush of liquid soothed her burning throat, spread a wave of calm through her. She wiped her face with the back of a hand and trudged back into the room.

Ara stood there wringing her hands. "Are you okay?"

"Yes." She sighed. "No, but I will be."

"Let me send for some lunch."

"I'm sorry. I have lost my appetite," Maya said. "I'd really like to lie down for a bit."

Misery screwed up Ara's face as she nodded and padded to the door.

"I'm not a spy, nor am I trying to marry into the royal family," Maya said to her back. "And I definitely didn't want to cause trouble between your brothers."

"They'll get over their pissing contest." Ara stood still in the open doorway. "Do you care about Akshay?"

All the reasons why she shouldn't, or couldn't, ran through her mind. In the end only the distilled truth remained. "Yes."

"Then do what your heart tells you is right." With that, the princess stepped out and shut the door.

Maya stared at the wooden expanse shutting her away from the rest of the castle and thought about the man, the life, she couldn't have.

Akshay flexed his aching hands as he stalked down the corridor. Jazz was damn lucky he was still in one piece—beaten and bruised perhaps, but still one piece. He'd heal. He shouldn't have spoken to Maya like that, and he definitely shouldn't have touched her.

He stopped and stared at the closed door of his room. She was on the other side of it. His heartmate. The one perfect soul that paired with his.

He'd suspected it the night before as he'd watched her sleep, but the encounter with Jazz had cemented it. Akshay wanted to charge in and claim her, but he hesitated as he remembered the look of horror plastered on Maya's face just before she'd fled. He didn't want to frighten her away. So he pulled in calming breaths and tried to tamp down the rage still swirling inside him like a hot desert wind. He needed to be calm, reasonable and persuasive. He needed her to stay.

She lay on her stomach, clutching his pillow in her arms. Wary golden eyes watched him approach the bed. "You look like shit."

Pulling on all his reserve, Akshay managed to stop a few feet from her. He touched the tenderness around his left eye and winced. Yeah, Jazz had landed a few good licks as well. Quick as a serpent, that one. "It was a fair fight."

"One you needn't have had."

"I guess I'm not as forgiving as you are." No one, *no one* insulted his woman. He wasn't an idiot. He knew she was hiding something and wished she'd trust him enough to share her secrets. But he loved her, and that meant accepting what she was ready to give.

They stared at each other in silence as he tried to find the words to propose to her, ask her to share his life. Damn, he'd always known he'd marry someday...yet, he never expected to be this nervous. Truth be told, he'd never expected to feel anything other than resigned acceptance.

She sat up in bed and tugged her dress into place. "I'm well enough to travel now," she said. "I'd appreciate it if you could have someone drop me off at a crossroad."

Temper and misery flared at her words, ate at him in ravenous bites. He firmed his stance and folded his arms across his chest to keep from grabbing and shaking some sense into her. "Prove it."

"What?"

"You look like a tough gal, someone who could handle ruffians on the road," he said. "You claim to be well enough to travel. Prove it and I will let you go with a clear conscience." *Never.*

Maya clambered out of the bed, consternation knitting her brows. "How?"

"Beat me in friendly combat."

Hope shone in her eyes. "If I win, I can leave?"

He nodded. "If I win, you stay."

"You want a fight, you'll get a fight." A fierce grin lit her face, as she rolled and loosened her shoulders. "Bring it on."

Heat and adrenaline rushed through Akshay, shot to his groin. Oh yes, he liked this woman. A woman with lean muscles and sexy curves, who wore her scars with pride and relished a good fight. A woman after his own heart. He sauntered toward the door and beckoned her with a wave. "Follow me."

CHAPTER 10

He led her out the door, to the gym on the next level. Only he, Jazz and their instructors used this place, sometimes inviting sparring partners and guests. It was considered an honor to be selected from among the royal guards. Akshay held his bracelet up and the door slid open with a soft swish.

Maya stepped into the room and gasped. Her head swiveled as she checked out all the weapons mounted and ready on the walls. From mighty hammers and javelins to jeweled daggers and everything in between. He was pleased to note the admiration in her gaze.

"So what are we fighting with?"

He laughed. "None of these," he said. "I meant friendly and not too dangerous, like hand-to-hand combat."

She pursed her full lips and he had the mad desire to kiss away her disappointment. Instead he stalked over to the rubber matting on the center of the floor. "Coming?"

"Hell, yeah," she said. "But first I need to change into something more practical." With a snap she was dressed in a skintight suit, leggings and boots. A padded vest hid her curves. Maya twisted her hair up in knot. "Aren't you going to need any protection?"

"I don't think so."

She shrugged and joined him on the mat, shifted into a ready stance.

Akshay stretched his neck, bones cracking in place. He met and held her gaze. They circled each other, watching, measuring. Then he leapt forward, wrapping her in an iron grip.

She countered with a head butt. The pain ricocheted from his chin to his brain as his head snapped back. Cursing, his hold loosened and he let her drop to the floor. She seized the opportunity to run him into the wall.

"Oof!" He grappled with her to block her hits and tried to find a hold on her bucking, squirming body. After about fifteen seconds, he found purchase and lurched around so that their positions were reversed. He managed to grab hold of both her hands and held them above her head with one of his. She tried to kick him, so he pressed his body to hers until she could hardly move. She panted beneath him with her full lips parted. It took all his control to keep from kissing her, from following the lead of his twitching cock.

"Just say enough, and I'll let you go."

"How about two out of three rounds?"

"Sure." He loosened his hold, preparing to step back. She smashed her heel down on his right foot.

"Ow!" Before he could take the next breath, she clipped him with an elbow, shoved him down on the mat and straddled him, pinning both his arms down.

She grinned down into his face. His gaze followed a rivulet of sweat sliding down her neck and disappearing in the channel between her breasts, pushed together by the suit. He forgot to breathe, think, move. His blood raced, every nerve in his body ached for her.

"Say enough, and I will let *you* go."

Her taunt goaded his competitive nature and galvanized Akshay into action. He bucked under Maya and threw her off. They rolled and wrestled on the floor, writhing and squirming against each other. Grappling and blocking.

Maya's hair came undone and spilled all over them. He caught a whiff of the faint Jasmine scent and stilled. She flipped and pinned him again.

Akshay didn't mind. Her hair curtained them off into an intimate seclusion, a moment taut with unspoken wants, where it was just him and her. Their ragged breaths mingled between them. His heart pounded as he drank Maya in, her molten gold eyes sparking with spirit, her generous mouth begging to be kissed.

"I believe this is the second time I have pinned you."

He swallowed and wet his lip with his tongue. "Then you must claim me and declare your victory."

"And how would I do that?" she whispered.

In answer, he raised his head off the floor, brought his mouth just shy of hers.

She claimed his mouth with hers, confident and in control. Tasted him in slow sucks and swirls. Pulled back.

With a slow glide of her tongue, she traced his silky lower lip, then scraped it with her teeth, teasing and worrying. Then backed off again. Her tongue flirted with his, swirling one moment, flicking and flying the next.

Akshay arched up from the floor with a hungry growl and pressed into the kiss, gave it his all. She melted against him, her hands loosening their hold, sliding around his head. He wrapped her in his iron grip and rolled over, pinning her beneath, kissing her over and over.

He craved her with every fiber of his being. He craved her touch, her taste, her scent. He craved her with a powerful hunger that could only be satisfied by his mate.

CHAPTER 11

Oh damn. Akshay was all over her. His hands, his mouth, his hair—every amazing bit of him—touched her, worked her until her heart revved and a desperate need for him rose within her like a siren call. She grew wet, hot and tingly. Her hips, her entire body, rose and undulated against him, dancing to a silent tune. She sighed and returned his kisses, his touches.

Maya couldn't even recall when they'd vanished their clothes, but she was glad of it as she skimmed and kissed his damp flesh and flexing muscles. Tasted his salty skin and inhaled his heady scent of sunshine and musk.

In return, his hands raced across her in rough urgency. Kneading and squeezing, fingers stopping for a slow pinch, a soft caress, nails scraping across her skin making her almost jitter out of her human body. Akshay flicked his tongue across her erect nipples, blew on their wet surface, and then clamped his hot, hungry mouth over one breast and suckled her hard. Obliterated all thought beyond desire.

Oh damn, oh damn, oh damn. What would it be like to remove all barriers, to join with him completely, essence with essence? Maya bit down on her tongue and sucked in a breath to distance herself from her dangerous thoughts. A moment's respite, then their bodies took over. Mouth sought mouth, hands sought flesh.

The room grew hot, shimmered, with the buildup of power fueled by need. Every cell in her body grew taut as agitated atoms pushed for release. Wildness stirred her essence to desperate heights. Both she and Akshay glowed with an ethereal light.

Her name burst from him on a ragged breath. Then he pulled back and held himself above her, panting, balancing on straining hands. He looked her in the eyes. "Maya, these last few days —"

Unease and anticipation raced down her spine. She pressed her fingers to his mouth. "Sshh, no—"

He nipped at her fingers, nudged them away. "Let me speak, or I will regret it forever."

Her breath lodged in her throat, her heart followed.

"These last few days with you have changed me."

"How?"

"Made me look at my life and realize what's been missing, made me find what I once thought was impossible."

She should shove him off and get out. Or reach up and pull him into a kiss. Either way, she should stop listening to his dangerous words. "What did you find?"

"I found you, my heartmate." He dropped a soft kiss on her mouth. "I want to join with you, soul to soul."

"But, but that's impossible."

"I know." He rested his forehead against hers, an unruly curl of hair brushed her skin. "It's okay. I love you for who you are, what you are."

He placed a kiss at the hollow of her throat.

Love? Panic unfurled deep in her gut. "What I am?"

"Hybrid, half djinn and half human. You may not be able to shift, but you complete me." Butterfly kisses landed along her jaw.

Relief and bitterness seeped into her. Oh, that old lie again. Maya wished she could tell Akshay the truth, but he couldn't bear to hear anything about the water djinns. And there were too many unanswered questions about what was going on between the two realms. "You're a crown prince. Your parents, your kingdom, your people will never accept a hybrid."

He held her gaze again. "It isn't for them to accept. The question is will *you* accept me?" He took a deep breath and let it out. "I'm willing to give up the crown to have you in my life."

Stunned, she stared at his hard warrior face, into those warm, chocolate eyes that held both fear and hope. Also, love. Part of her wanted to sink into this dream, make it her reality. But would the love remain once he found out what she truly was, a princess of the water djinns?

A wistful smile touched his face and sadness shaded his eyes. "You don't feel the same about me."

"I don't know how I feel." *Liar.*

His lips curved up a notch. He waggled his brows. "Well, then I better get back to convincing."

His fingers explored her skin with soft strokes, his mouth laid a trail of hot kisses. The rough brush of his stubble-covered chin, the soft caress of his hair, aroused every nerve ending in her body. Need zipped through her essence, rocked her body.

He said her name over and over like a mantra as he touched her, kissed her, stroked her. She bowed off the floor, into him, in response…giving herself up to the magic he wove. Her eyes fluttered closed and scenes from their candle-lit bath flitted through her mind. Of all things, she remembered him gently washing her hair, untangling the knots. Him carrying her to bed and tucking her in. Akshay spooning against her back, holding her safe and warm in his arms through the night.

With a sigh, she stretched and gave herself over to the liquid desire spilling thick and sweet through her veins. Let herself drown in the storm created by their want.

"Maya, heartmate," he whispered against her ear, sending shivers spiraling through her. "I need you, I need you so bad." One hand slid down until fingers explored her core, wet and hot. Aching to be filled.

"Akshay, I need you," she gasped. "I need you now." Tension tightened her body as every inch of her demanded satisfaction.

He pulled her against him roughly. "Patience, sweet Maya."

"Now," she returned in a half-crazed whisper. "Please, please now."

His mouth crushed hers in a demanding kiss. His fingers continued to tweak and tease the whorl of nerves hidden by her nether lips. Desire ripped through her body making her moan and writhe, burned away all rational thought.

"Akshay, heartmate," she whispered against his mouth. "I need you."

"And you have me, all of me."

A cry escaped her throat as his erection, thick and hard, pushed inside her, filled her. She tightened her arms around him, rode him as he rode her, marrying their rhythm.

Her hunger for him, now awakened, refused to be slaked. Instead it grew and built like an out of control flood, rushed through her fast and powerful, destroying everything that stood in its way. He matched her urgency with desperation and drove into her like a djinn possessed.

Waves of sensation washed over her, crashed through her defenses. She stared into his dark intense eyes. Time slowed until she was only aware of his eyes and the scream building inside her. Tension notched tighter, and tighter.

The scream tore from her throat at the same time as Akshay came, she unraveled as his hot seed shot through her. All barriers between them disappeared. His essence, like motes of sunshine, floated above hers for a time. Her essence glowed silver like a mist created from moonlight, and reached for his. Then the two joined and sank into each other.

A river of emotions and memories rushed over and around Maya, drowning her in Akshay's life. The fast and fierce current dragged her through image after image. A sharp-faced man laughing, Nijhoom forest, a familiar battlefield, a midnight horse, water wraiths, rhakshas, earth djinns, the clash of weapons. Screams filled her head, and the hot tang of blood filled her nostrils. Loss wrapped her in its cold embrace.

Maya's stomach quivered as more images crashed over her like waves. Herself in full battle gear lying in the mud, the dark shadow of an air assassin, the young man again, but this time he held a bloody sword and wore a grim mask, a flash of silver, the young man's headless body tumbling to the ground. Guilt and regret wrapped around her like a tangle of seaweed and pulled her under.

She gasped for air and fought to free herself, but the images and emotion kept striking and battering her like driftwood and debris. Suddenly, there she was laughing on the flying carpet, asleep and tangled in his sheets, and then awake and staring, lips parted, eyes bright, with naked need glowing on her face. A soft whisper: *Akshay, heartmate*.

Akshay shoved her away with rough hands and held her at arm's length. Maya lay panting on the sweaty mat, staring at the blur of Akshay's wide-eyed face. A panicked pounding burst into the room. She blinked and pulled in a sharp breath, as if emerging from deep underwater. Knowledge seeped into her consciousness. Knowledge that something undeniable and awful awaited her.

An avalanche of images tumbled down on Akshay, left him gasping for breath with bands of pain constricting his chest. None of it made sense. A blue woman suiting up for battle, hugging and laughing with other blue women, metamorphosing into an ugly, hulking rhaksha, then himself, terrible in his metal armor, raising his sword. In a rush of moments, he'd tasted both love and fear.

Then more of him caught in intimate detail—from the veining on the back of his hands, to the hunger glittering in his dark eyes. Along with those images came waves of confusion, frustration, guilt and love. An infernal pounding hurt his muddled head. Worse, a sense of loss infused him, left him hurting.

Akshay blinked and stared at the woman who completed him, who had lied to him. Beautiful and naked, skin the blue of a robin's egg. The woman from the battlefield, a water djinn, his enemy. His gaze searched the familiar face of his beloved, trying to make sense of the change. "Maya?"

The door broke open with a crash and soldiers charged in. The sound of splintering wood and heavy steps banged around his head. Rough hands grabbed him, her, pulled them apart. He shivered at the loss of her warmth.

His father glared at him.

"Just as we suspected, a spy," Jazz crowed.

The buzz of voices filled his head, words crashed into each other, didn't make sense. He looked around until his gaze collided with hers. But then soldiers came between them and hid Maya from view. She screamed his name as she was dragged from the room. Akshay struggled to get to her, to fight off the soldiers holding him down. Rage whipped through him, but joining with her had cost him, left him too weak. "Maya!"

His cry earned him a slap. "You're acting like a fool," the king shouted. "Pull yourself together."

"Bring her back!" He demanded, and then resorted to a plea. "Please, bring her back."

"Forget about her," the king said. "She's nothing but a liar and a spy."

She was a liar. He couldn't deny that. She'd lied to him from the very first and apparently continued to lie to him. Her blue face floated in his mind. A water djinn. Bitterness swept through him as the realization settled inside. Yet, his heart had recognized her as his mate. And that was a truth he couldn't deny, despite the sick churning in his gut. Akshay shook his head. "She's my heartmate."

His father sighed as pity flooded his eyes. "Heartmates are just pretty fancies that women spin," he said. "Forget those silly stories of your mother. Royalty marries to cement alliances and strengthen power, to claim a son."

Akshay stared at the man he called Father, the man he'd looked up to all his life.

"She played you for a fool, son." His father's voice turned gruff. "She's nothing but a whore and a spy."

Rage rumbled through him at the words. And for the first time he saw only a king and a stranger. A man he could no longer respect nor obey. A man he wanted to pulverize.

In the next instant, shame wrapped him in an oily shroud, made him hang his head. His father had always wanted the best of him and for him. Maya had lied, turned out to be the enemy. Perhaps the king was right. Perhaps she had used him.

Akshay, heartmate. His treacherous memory replayed her words. *I need you.*

Resolve hardened inside him. Perhaps everything between them had been nothing more than a convenient fancy, but he needed to hear it from Maya. They owed each other at least that.

"I need to talk to her." He raised his head. "Let me go to her."

"Lock him in his room," his father ordered and then stormed from the gym.

CHAPTER 12

From the crown prince's bedroom to the royal dungeon—her life sucked.

Maya huddled on the narrow cot and looked around at the gray stone walls of her tiny cell. The cold made her bones ache and she pulled the scratchy blanket tighter. Nausea churned in her gut as she breathed in the damp, musty air. She stared at the barred window up high on the wall, letting in the sound of rain, and yearned to be outside.

Akshay hadn't come. They'd served her three meals—none of which she'd eaten—so she supposed the entire day had passed. And he hadn't come. Emptiness sulked in her heart. She shouldn't have expected him. Their relationship—if it could be called that—had been built on lies. Yes, he'd professed his love to her...but he didn't even know her. She'd lied to him from day one and she couldn't blame him for not coming.

Her last glimpse of Akshay haunted her. His strong, square-jawed face crumpled in confusion, eyes wide with dark horror. His emotions—numb denial, burning anger, guilt and bitter betrayal—had ripped through her like steel-tipped arrows, left her bleeding.

Maya wrapped her arms tight around her body, around the tiny life flickering inside, as she rocked back and forth. Tears flooded her, turning her insides into soggy mush, wanting to pour out. She sniffled and dug her nails into her flesh, trying to hold in the tears. She mustn't. She was stronger than that. Damn it, she was one of the fiercest water djinn warriors of Shagaard.

A soft coo drew her attention back to the window. The sight of the mourning dove that flew in moments later to perch on the cot made her jerk to her feet. Umber finished her transformation and rushed to hug Maya. "What happened?"

I had the best damn sex of my life and transformed to the form closest to my nature. "I don't know," she said, pulling in a deep whiff of the sweet jasmine scent. "I ended up revealing my true form."

Umber's gaze fell to the floor and she curled her lips in distaste. "Yes, I heard. You turned out to be the water djinn spy everyone feared."

"No!" Maya clutched at her only possible friend in all of Bhramadesh. "Yes, I'm a water djinn, but I'm not a spy. Believe me, I had never intended to come here." The tears rushed from her then. "Life just snowballed and now I'm a prisoner."

Umber looked away and, after a moment, nodded. "Even though I have no proof, I believe you." She wiped away Maya's tears. "I have been life's plaything too often not to."

The question that had been gnawing inside jumped out. "How's Akshay?"

Umber threw up her hands and huffed out a breath. "The men have been holed up in closed council since this morning," she said. "They're probably planning war on the water djinns."

Maya dropped onto the cot. "Oh no, there's going to be war all because of me," she wailed. "Please, you have to help me out of here. I have to try and stop this."

Umber's eyes rounded and her hands fluttered in front of her. "Me? How can I get you out of a locked cell?"

Maya glared at the metal door that separated her from freedom. "I'm a water djinn, I can squeeze through," she said. A twinge of panic spread through her. She'd be risking the baby, but these were desperate times. "But I don't know your country very well, so if someone could just get me to a crossroad."

The queen shook her head at her words. "No, as soon as you use magic like that, they'll sense it and come running," she said and pursed her lips. After a moment, she spoke again. "Why don't you just tell them you are pregnant? My friend, the healer, will come forward to support you."

A smile lit Umber's face as the idea took root. "That would solve your problems," she said. "This family prizes its sons."

Akshay's face as he whispered her name, called her his heartmate, rose in her mind and her breath hitched. If she had to marry, he'd be the one…but not like this. He probably hated her now, but he'd still do the right thing. She wouldn't force herself on him. Fresh tears scratched at the corner of her eyes.

Maya shook her head. "No."

"Don't be foolish," Umber said. "They'll take you out of the prison and marry you to the crown prince. What more could you ask for?"

She hugged herself again. What if there was another child and what if that one was a girl? Even though she'd been misinformed about much of the earth djinn world, the women existed in the shadows. Maya met Umber's gaze. "Answer me truly, if you had a choice...would you have raised your son in the royal court here or amongst your clan? What if you had a daughter?"

Umber turned away to look up at the window. "My people could never equal the richness, the power my son has here," she said. "But I wish he could have known my clan as I did." Her head sank low to her breast. "And I thank the Creator I didn't give birth to a daughter here."

Maya seized her hands. "I beg of you, one woman to another, please help me get out," she said. "I just want to return to my people and have my baby at home."

This time Umber's eyes glistened with unshed tears. "But I will get into trouble if I help you escape."

"No, no you won't," she said, not letting go. "Just tell them I forced you to or something. Please."

Umber pressed her lips together into a thin, rigid line. At last she nodded. "Let me think of a way," she said. "I'll be back."

"Promise?"

"Promise."

Maya's breath stuttered in her lungs as the other woman's hand slipped from her grasp. She had no choice but to trust Umber. If the queen didn't return by tomorrow afternoon, she'd take matters into her own hands, risk everything to escape.

Akshay stood by the window and stared at the rain. It was as if the sky had crashed open and all the water in the heavens drummed down in a heavy, wet downpour. He breathed in the beautiful wet earth scent wafting in the cool breeze, as a thin film of rain spattered his clothes and ran down his skin. A calm descended on him. After almost a ten-year drought, it was raining. A good, hard rain. Anything was possible.

The door unlocked behind him and soft footsteps entered. Akshay didn't bother to turn.

"You okay?" Jazz asked.

"It's raining."

His brother joined him at the window, stuck out a hand into the welcome wetness. "Yes, it started just about when you both—um, screamed."

He wiped his hand with his handkerchief, and then carefully folded it and returned it to his breast pocket. They stood in silence for a bit.

"Why were you and the soldiers at the door?"

Jazz shot him a quick glance. "You were being watched, and when you took her to the gym, amongst all those weapons...Father was worried about you." He cleared his throat. "Nobody wanted you to get hurt."

Father. Hurt. Was a stab wound any worse than this feeling of confusion and emptiness that engulfed him since Maya was snatched away? "Is he still cursing me out?"

"He and the council would like to talk to you," Jazz said. "If you're ready."

Akshay nodded. He'd concluded that ranting and raging wouldn't get him what he wanted. Since he was the crown prince, he needed to act like one. Calm, commanding and in control. He changed into a fresh outfit. The heavily decorated dress uniform he wore to the crowning. Combing fingers through his hair, he turned to Jazz. "As ready as I will ever be."

CHAPTER 13

They marched along the balconies in silence, enjoying the damp refreshing breeze, and then delved into the twisting, turning corridors leading further and further underground. Akshay set a quick pace; he'd already wasted too much time wrapping his head around the fact that Maya was a water djinn, trying to give her up, and forget. Jazz knocked, opened the door and announced him.

Akshay strode in, head held high, and greeted everyone with brief nods. "Gentlemen."

The king glowered at him. "Have you come to your senses?"

"I'm here, aren't I?"

His father stared at him for a long moment. "How are you doing?"

"I'm well." He delivered a short bow. "Thank you for asking, your Majesty."

The king shuffled the papers in front of him, tapped them together and laid them to the side. Akshay pulled out the end chair, at the opposite end from him, and sat.

"We all agree, the water djinns need a response," the king said. "First thing tomorrow we will send a messenger to the Emperor of all Djinns requesting his military response. A messenger will also be sent to Shagaard, to the King and Queen of the water djinns, informing them that one of theirs has been caught spying in our courts. We will offer to exchange her for a more favorable water deal."

He paused to sip from a glass of water at his hand. "If they fail to meet our demands, the prisoner will be executed and we go to war."

A wave of bitter revulsion swept through Akshay. His father meant to use Maya, the woman he loved, as a pawn. Didn't see her as anything more. He swallowed his ire and stood. "You all have agreed?"

"Yes." His father stared down the table. No one moved. "We saw no other course."

"That's very shortsighted of you." Akshay held his gaze. "I'm the crown prince, the future ruler of this country, so I have to consider the big picture."

The councilors leaned forward on the table.

"Are you all enjoying the rain?"

Heads nodded and smiles lit up faces. "It's a blessing," Councilman Heggi said. "A miracle."

"Jazz tells me it began to rain as soon as I joined spirit to spirit with Maya."

"You have no proof, it's just crazy coincidence," the king sputtered.

"A ruler cannot afford to believe in coincidences or craziness, Sire." He looked around the table. "Has anyone bothered to consult our mages?"

Councilman Achmed spoke up. "I did." His gaze darted around in nervous dance, but then he sat up straight in his chair. "Even though our mages have only limited powers, I thought it was important to consult them in the event of such importance. The rain."

"And what did they say?"

"They most definitely felt water magic at work." He tugged at his ear lobe. "And they pinpointed your location as its source."

"Which makes complete sense," Akshay spread his hands out agreeably. "The intimate joining of djinn heartmates has its own powerful magic. Our ancestors have written about it, and generations after generations have passed those stories down."

"Women's stories." The king snorted.

"It was powerful enough to make Maya reveal herself, and to make it rain."

"Do you have a plan, Crown Prince?" Heggi asked.

"Yes." Akshay smiled. "I plan to marry Maya."

Stunned silence greeted his words.

The king paled as he grabbed the table with both hands and half-rose from his chair. "What?"

"We have trod the path of war for too long," Akshay said. "It's time to try something different. We need water, and the water djinns control water. Marriage would cement us together into the perfect alliance."

Jazz smiled. "Brilliant. I wonder why we haven't tried that before?"

"Because," their father's voice sounded hoarse and shaky, as if weighed down by years of living. "Water djinns, especially the women, cannot be trusted."

Akshay blinked. Was his father repeating long-held prejudice? Or was there more to it? He leaned forward wondering if he'd imagined the pain edging the words.

"Maya's had plenty of opportunities to harm me, but she never has," he said. "Moreover, she's brought us rain. How is that untrustworthy?"

"They are more cunning than that." The king rubbed his face with both hands as if trying to erase the unpleasant thoughts inside his head. "Your grandmother was a water djinn."

Jazz and Akshay exchanged a quick look. "Your mother? Who died giving birth to you?"

The king sighed and slumped into his chair. "She didn't die." His voice quivered. "She ran away, abandoned my father and me."

"I never knew we had water djinn in the family," Jazz said.

"Because she's only existed as a name in the book of genealogy, mentioned twice—at marriage and at childbirth-slash-pseudo-death," Akshay blurted.

A soft groan escaped the king. Akshay's heart faltered as he noticed the wrinkles mapping the ashen skin, the drooping shoulders, the stillness. He walked toward his father.

"Women's lineages are unimportant." Heavy breaths puffed out the King's chest. "And her name, her story, her very existence deserves to be forgotten. She took a human mage, a guest at our courts, as lover and ran away with him."

"How old were you?" Akshay asked, standing next to his chair. Damn, his father had a bald spot. How the hell hadn't he noticed it before?

"Three."

Ah, shit. The king was about five centuries old now…and pain still resonated in his words.

Akshay clasped his father's shoulder. "I'm sorry you had to live through that," he said. "And I'm sorry you were hurt."

He squatted down so he could look into his father's face. "Maya is not the same."

The king opened his eyes. Their dark depths shone with emotion. "I don't want you to get hurt." He glanced over at Jazz. "Either of you."

Akshay bit his lip and nodded. "Not having Maya in my life will hurt more than anything else."

His father sighed again. "Then go to her," he said. "Good luck and blessings."

Grinning like a fool, Akshay shot to his feet and raced from the room. Applause rang in his ears, heralded him out. As he ran he imagined Maya's face when he rescued her, shared the good news. Her absence was like an ache in his bones. Creator, he was going to cover her face with kisses.

As he neared her cell, he heard a voice, so hoarse that it was difficult to discern it as female, calling for help, to be let out. Alarm spread through him. She'd seemed so tough. What had they done to her to make her so desperate? He picked up speed until he reached the guard on duty.

The guard dropped the comic he was reading and jumped to his feet. "Good morning sire!"

"Don't you hear that?" He pointed down the corridor toward the cell where the cries came from.

The djinn's gaze darted down the corridor and back. He shrugged. "All new prisoners beg to be let out."

CHAPTER 14

Akshay snatched up the keys from the table. "Which one of these unlocks her cell?"

A shaky finger pointed in reply and Akshay ran to the door. He reached out to her mind to mind and only received panicked static in return. *I'm coming.*

The door unlocked with a squeal. "Careful, I'm opening the door."

He shoved it open and rushed in to face the tear-streaked face of his stepmother. Usually a cool woman, she threw herself at him and clutched his arms. "Thank you!"

"What are you doing in here?"

"She—she tricked me." A sob shuddered through Umber's slender frame. "She pulled me in and rushed out the door. Slamming it shut on me."

Akshay looked from the woman to the door and back. Maya would definitely be strong enough, and perhaps desperate enough. Throwing her in the cell had been such a bad idea. "Where did she go?"

"I—I don't know," Umber sniffled as she gathered the dried branches of herbs that lay spilled at her feet.

"Where was the guard? Why didn't he stop her?"

"Oh, she grabbed my shawl as she ran out," Umber said. "Maybe he thought it was me."

He extricated himself from her and hurried to the door, only to stop at the threshold. "Wait, why did you come down to see her?"

"A woman in her condition needs special care. I was just bringing her some herbs to put in her drinking water."

He narrowed his eyes at her. Had the soldiers hurt Maya when they brought her down here? "A woman in her condition?"

Her gaze skittered away from him.

"What condition?"

"She's carrying your child, a son." The words hurtled out of Umber.

He stared at her, drained of all feeling for a moment. "What?"

"Um, yes. You know I can tell."

A breath rushed out of him as he stumbled against the doorjamb. "Heaven and Hell! She's pregnant."

In two strides, Akshay stood in front of Umber, his fingers digging into her arms. "She's pregnant and on the run?" He took a deep breath and argued himself from shaking the woman. "Tell me where she went."

"I don't know," Umber said. "Probably to the nearest crossroads. She said something about needing to make it to Nijhoom Forest."

Shit. His insides churned. He'd intended to never return to that Creator-forsaken place again, to the site of Patthar's death. But if Maya was headed there, he had to go. Maybe he could catch her before she got too far.

Akshay released Umber and fled out the door. "Tell Father and Jazz I'm going after Maya."

Dizziness gripped Akshay as he zipped through the ether faster than usual. First he rode Midnight to the nearest crossroads, right next to the Ration Center in the marketplace. The soldiers guarding the crossroads reported only merchants had traveled through since morning. All with proper paperwork. No single female. Blue or otherwise.

Had Maya snuck into some rich trader's caravan? He wouldn't underestimate her. With a deep breath, he pulled invisibility around him and Midnight and traveled on.

Akshay swallowed and used his mind to search for Maya. Of course, she'd be invisible but he should be able to sense her djinn vibration, recognize her heart. Nothing. He nudged Midnight with his heels and continued through to the land of the water djinns.

Wide-eyed, he goggled at the plain at the outer edge of water djinn territory. A soft carpet of new grass covered the rolling expanse, dotted with wildflowers of every color imaginable. Was this truly the bone dry land he'd led Patthar and his army across a mere two weeks ago?

He breathed in the sweet air and tried to tamp down the bitterness welling inside him. Had the water djinns washed away all signs of the war with cleansing rain, or was this new life flourishing thanks to all the blood and death that had soaked into the earth?

Midnight took the opportunity to lower his head and taste the verdant grass. Akshay closed his eyes and pulled in another deep breath, exhaled. Life ended in death, followed by new life. That was the natural cycle.

Maya's face, her golden eyes glazed with liquid languor and lips parted in a sexy smile, filled his mind. *Maya.* She'd given him the greatest gift—life. She'd taken a man drowning in sorrow and guilt and made him come alive. She was carrying his child, the new life they'd made together. The realization shook through him like an earthquake, crumbled the remaining walls to dust. He needed to find his heartmate and his son.

Akshay muttered a short prayer for all the souls who'd returned to the earth at the battle, and then scanned the horizon. Nijhoom Forest still hulked, dark and forbidding, at the other end of the plain. Where was she?

Awareness of her presence swept over him like cool, gentle rain. He could scent her in the air. A dark flicker almost at the edge of the forest snagged his attention, and his heart somersaulted. He spurred Midnight into a run and raced toward her.

CHAPTER 15

Hoof beats thundered behind Maya, made her whip around. Akshay bore down on her, his gaze burning hot, his face tight and hard with determination. Oh Creator, he looked pissed, and magnificent. A sob hitched at her throat. She was almost to the forest, almost home. Even though her heart pulled toward Akshay, she broke into a run.

"Maya!" His shout lashed her from behind, made her run harder. Breath sawed through her lungs, leaving behind a burning ache.

"Hiyaah!" Hoof beats drowned out her panicked heartbeat, shook the ground beneath her feet, drew closer. He passed her in a great rush of musky hot air and wheeled to a stop in her path, between her and Shagaard. A cloud of dust and debris flew into the air, spattered her skin. Maya stumbled to a stop as coughs wracked her body.

Akshay leapt from the horse and landed in front of her. "We need to talk."

"I'm a water djinn and you're an earth djinn." Tears streamed down her face. She straightened her spine. "There's nothing to discuss."

"Like hell there isn't." He grabbed her and kissed her, thoroughly blowing her senses. Oh damn, he tasted good. So good. She kissed him back, matching his fierce claim with her own.

When they parted, her lips stung and yet she was bereft and wanted more. Maya licked her lips and stared at him. He stood glittering like the sun in his white and gold dress uniform. She shuffled her feet, ashamed of her sack-like peasant disguise. "We fought each other."

"We also made love."

A wave of heated memories rushed over her, left her burning.

"Did you come to Bhramadesh to spy?"

"You're the one who dragged me there!"

"You lied to me." His voice slid soft and silky across her skin.

"Yes." Heat crawled up her neck and face. "I'm sorry, I didn't have a choice."

"Yes, you did." He stepped close again and his intense gaze made her shiver. "You could have trusted me."

Oh damn. How could he make her feel like chocolate about to be devoured and a sorry disappointment all at the same time? Shame welled up inside, washed away all words.

"Worse, you left me." He closed the gap between them. His heat wrapped around her. "You ran away."

"Your people threw me in a dungeon!" She huffed out a breath.

"I was working things out," he said. "You should have trusted me and waited."

Anger seared her thoughts. "Sorry, I'm not good at waiting around to be rescued."

His eyes narrowed to slits. "Given that you're pregnant, running away all by yourself wasn't the most intelligent thing to do."

Maya flinched at his words, wrapped her arms around her stomach. He knew. Oh damn, he knew.

"I didn't want to have my baby in Bhramadesh, among earth djinns." He paled at her words, the corners of his mouth tightened. She took a hasty breath and continued. "I wanted to be with my family."

"The child you're carrying is *our* baby," he said. "I love you. We could have worked something out."

Her heart pounded in her throat. She couldn't deny his words. "I'm sorry," she whispered. "I was scared."

He wrapped her in his arms and held her tight. "So was I. I was terrified I'd lose you, our son, our new life." He kissed the top of her head.

Clapping startled them out of each other's arms. "Oh, this is perfect."

Umber's pale eyes glittered with a mad joy. Her lips, painted red, twisted in a vicious smile. Ten air djinns, dressed in the black robes and masks of assassins, hovered in a half-circle around her, fluttering and flickering in suspension, waiting to let all hell turn loose.

Umber? What was she doing here? Maya stared at the woman as nausea washed over her and realization dawned.

"Go." Akshay pushed Maya behind him. The earth quaked and cracked as he transformed to his djinn form. His pretty uniform split at the seams and tore as he grew taller and broader, his skin turned from human to burnished gold. Muscles bulged and came together creating a giant made of glowing, pulsing rocks.

The assassins rushed him, slashing and swirling with all kinds of weapons. With a roar, Akshay charged into them. He raised rocks and stones with his earth magic and hurled them at his opponents.

Now was her chance. She stared at the trees, only a dash away. Once she entered the forest, seeped into the ground, she could travel the root system and go home. Her hands rubbed her belly. The intelligent thing would be to go for help.

The sun flashed and glittered off the swords, spears and chains the assassins wielded. They shadowed and let the barrage of rocks pass through them without a scratch. If Akshay managed to throw off one assassin, two more attacked. If he turned to take care of them, another few ran in from different sides. Red blood, so bright that it hurt her eyes, ran down his body. She wouldn't get back in time to save him.

"I'm not running away again," she said. Pulling in a deep breath, she focused her mind.

Denidra, Mother, water djinns, I need you. Hoping she'd been heard, Maya turned her attention to do what she could on her own. *Trees of Nijhoom forest, I need your water.*

She turned her back to the fight, closed her eyes and stretched out her arms to the forest. With every breath and thought, she called water and magic to her, sucked with her soul. Maya's essence tingled, then vibrated and expanded as cool water flowed into her, charged her being. Magic swirled and sparked in her veins, magic from the water and the trees. Water foamed and frothed at her feet.

Maya opened her eyes and reveled in the silver glow of her body. With another breath, she let go and let the elements move her. She danced. Her arms wove and curled through the air, pulling the water at her fingertips into a jiggling, liquid ball.

Akshay fell to his knees, bowed his head, panting. His skin glowed red hot, cracked in places leaking out the liquid gold of his essence. An air assassin made the sign of the Creator, raised his axe.

"No!" Maya threw the water ball.

It hit the assassin in his midsection and broke. The axe flew out of his hands and traveled backwards. His group stood stunned for a moment, then rushed to finish Akshay. She threw water balls, one after another in rapid fire.

Her initial success in pushing them away was short lived. The air djinns picked themselves up, swerved and dodged her water balls and kept coming. She resorted to waves. They'd take a hell of lot more from her, but they'd be worth it. With great big swings of her arms, she sent waves racing toward the assassins.

Not so easy to avoid, the waves washed them back. Her heart cheered as Akshay stumbled to his feet, flexed his muscles and started throwing great big clods of earth. His earth and her water smashed together to cover the assassins with mud. Layer after layer. Their frenzied attack slowed as the mud weighed down their whirling robes. Hope flared. They just needed to bury the damn things in mud.

With a blood curdling yell, Umber charged with a raised sword. When had she gotten past Akshay? Maya turned sideways to avoid the attack, but not quickly enough. Sharp steel slashed through her sleeve and bit into her arm. Blood ran out, warm and wet.

Desperately, Maya hit Umber with a rush of water and sent her staggering. But it cost her, left her soul sucked dry and hurting. She searched her lumpy dress for a weapon. Nothing. Of course, Umber wouldn't have included one. Shit.

Umber swiped dripping limp hair her from her face and snarled. "You bitch!"

Oh damn. The crazy woman was pissed and armed. Maybe Maya could talk her down, change her mind. "I thought you were my friend."

"I helped you escape, I gave you a chance to get away from all this," Umber said, circling closer. "Too bad you stopped to chat."

Maya's breath came rough and ragged, leaving behind a trail of hurt in her lungs. She was running on empty. If she only had some time, some more water. "Why are you doing this?"

Umber scowled, her face ugly with hate. "I didn't put up with years of earth djinn shit to watch Akshay take the throne," she said. "My son will be king."

Warm rain fell to the earth. Maya basked in the soft kisses of raindrops. *We are coming Maya. We are with you.*

Maya dodged Umber's lunge, threw a bucket's worth of water at her feet. "He will still be trapped and part of that culture. You wanted him to know your clan, the freedom of the caravans."

Cursing, Umber wobbled and pulled herself out of the muddy skid. "My clan can only offer my son camels and dust. No, I have given him more, so much more. It's our destiny to be greater than my backwards clan." Anger drove the sword into the fleshy part of Maya's thigh. She cried out in pain.

Umber laughed. She withdrew the sword and attacked again. Maya pulled together a hasty shield of magic and deflected the blow. "But you will still be forgotten, hidden away in the women's domain."

"No!" Umber threw herself into the fight with renewed fire. "I will be the power behind the throne. I will have a place at court. I have brought up Jazz to be the better man, to put *me* first." She drove Maya back, almost into the forest.

The rain fell harder, stinging exposed skin, soaking into her. They danced around each other until Maya again saw the fight beyond.

Akshay gave a grunt of pain as a sword sank into his side. He dropped to his knees. The four remaining assassins swarmed over him like flies on a carcass. *No.* She had to get to him, and help. Save him and see where their life would lead. She swayed on her feet.

Umber glanced over at the fight and laughed again. The unfairness of the fight, the possibility of losing Shay, propelled Maya forward. She needed to get the sword away and knock the woman unconscious. She body slammed into Umber. Her leg burned, but she gritted her teeth and held on, tried to snatch the sword from Umber's death grip.

Snarling, Umber kneed her wounded leg. Again and again. Pain rocketed through Maya stealing her breath and leaving her weak. Her opponent tore out of her grasp and rolled away. For a moment, both women lay panting on the ground.

The wet earth slowly released moisture and magic into Maya's skin, and the skies above continued to rain down on her. Energy flowed into her from all directions, rocked through her in gentle waves.

Denidra, her mother, her father, her sisters and aunts, her grandmother, her people showered her in water magic. Their strength pooled together with earthier strands from Ara—what the hell was she doing here?—and Akshay.

Oh damn, he couldn't afford to share any of his magic with her. He needed it all to stay alive.

CHAPTER 16

Panicked, Maya mentally reached out to Akshay. *Stop! What are you doing?*

I couldn't save Patthar, but I can save you and our baby.

No!

Yes. You must live, live for me and our son.

No.

Go. Know that I love you.

Hell no. She couldn't let things end like this between them.

Umber charged again, sword ready to slash. The smile on her face made Maya tremble inside, but she forced herself to lie still, look defeated. Wait. Wait. Now.

At the last moment, when the queen was almost on top of her, Maya blasted her with all the new reserves. Umber flew back, but then her body shifted, melted, and joined with the ground until she stood as solid as a mountain. She laughed as the water magic flowed around her and away.

Her hands slashed and clawed the air and a barrage of pebbles and debris flew at Maya, bit into her skin. A rock hit her temple and forced out a cry. She threw her arms up in front of her body, but larger, sharper rocks continued pelting her, cutting into her skin. Tears ran down her face. Oh damn, she'd be stoned to death. She and the baby.

Stumbling, Maya focused herself and called her magic back. It turned like a giant anaconda made of water and wrapped in tight bands around Umber, immobilizing her.

Umber struggled and shrieked. "You can't stop me! You can't! You can't!" Each outburst was punctuated by a shove or a kick. Magic, bitter and black with hate, spilled out of her in great big clouds. Swirled, and flowed in the air like something alive.

Oily tendrils of magic wrapped around Maya, claiming her. Its acrid sting made her eyes water and her throat burn. Every breath hurt. Coughing and choking, Maya continued to tighten her hold.

An icy chill seeped through her skin and invaded her essence, freezing her. Maya gasped as cold ghostly fingers pushed inside her belly, reaching for the baby. Her mind screamed a silent warning. Umber had human magic, too. Maya clutched her arms about her midsection, but knew it wouldn't stop the queen, wouldn't protect her and Shay's child. "No," she said. "No."

Nausea churned through her, making her dizzy. Maya swallowed and tamped down the bile. No time to lose.

Desperate, Maya called on the Creator and dug deep inside. A fresh flood of power rushed and rumbled through her like a river breaking through a dam. Heavy and hard, almost solid, water magic blasted out, washed away the bindings of dark magic. Maya brought her hands together and forced the magic into a smooth and weighty spear. She hefted it and firmed her stance. She couldn't let Umber win.

"Akshay's whore!" The woman screamed. "Let me go no—"

Maya shoved the water magic down Umber's throat. The liquid force pressed the queen down into the ground, drowning her, smothering her screams and her breath until she lay limp and still.

Only then did Maya let go and drop to the ground. Magic, both dark and liquid, turned to dust and floated away on the air.

She'd given almost everything, and now her limbs felt soft and squishy, trembling at the slightest movement. Akshay. She had to get to Akshay. Depleted and half-crawling, she dragged herself through the mud toward him. Djinns milled around where she'd last seen him. Oh Creator, let him be alive.

Rough hands grabbed her and lifted her from the plain. She stared at Jazz's hard profile, into his gray eyes. So much like his mother.

He cradled her to his chest and broke into a run. "Shay's dying and asking for you."

Maya bit down on the fresh pain caused by every jolt and step. She had to get to Akshay. She loved him, and he needed to know.

Panting, Jazz gently lowered her next to Akshay. He lay slumped over, bleeding out in the mud, pulling in shallow rasping breaths. She grabbed a limp hand and squeezed. "Shay, I love you. I should have trusted you." Sobs hammered out of her body. "I need you. You have to stay alive for me and your son. I trust you, I know you can."

Maya. Heartmate. He opened his eyes and stared at her. She thought she saw stars and the universe in them, all the answers she'd ever sought.

A frail hand brushed the top of her head. "You love him."

Her grandmother's reedy voice had Maya's head snapping around. Her grandmother, once a renowned healer, hardly left her apartment, writing and reading in her retirement, sometimes spending times over tea and card games with her friends. But she was here. "Save him, please."

"We can try." Her grandmother looked around, let her gaze linger on the ashen face of the king. "You're Liana's son. I can see her in you."

The king's eyes brimmed with tears, and he nodded. "Save my son, please."

"Let's get them both to the healing center," her grandmother ordered in a crisp voice. Hands lifted her up, and pain bloomed again like a reopened wound. Maya moaned as she sank into unrelenting blackness.

The air smelled of rain, herbs and blood. Akshay lay in the dimly lit room, staring at dark shadows among the rafters above, and reminded himself he was in the water djinn healing center. He'd been floating in and out of consciousness for a while now…a surreal boat ride. Every time he'd managed to hold on for a few moments, he'd asked about Maya. The blue water djinn healers always smiled and assured him she was fine. He wanted to see her for himself, make sure.

Today he'd demand to be taken to her. The ancient healer padded into the room. "Oh you're awake!"

He found comfort in her familiar wrinkled face. It seemed like she'd been almost constantly by his side chanting, soothing, healing. "Thank you, for everything you have done."

She turned old, knowing eyes on him. "Yet, you want something more."

"I'd like to see Maya." Akshay held her gaze. "Please."

"Let's see how you're doing first," she said and placed a cool, dry palm across his forehead. "No fever."

"I need to talk to her."

"And there are plenty of people who want to talk to you."

He didn't want to talk to anyone else, just Maya. He clamped his mouth shut to hold back the whine, but his chin jutted out in mutiny.

"She's visited you several times."

"Really?" He sat up straighter. "Why didn't she wake me?"

"You needed to heal, just as now you need to talk to everyone," she said, checking his pulse. "There's a time and place for everything."

She walked out the door, only to return minutes later with several water djinns and earth djinns. Everyone was dressed in court attire. Apparently protocol had reverted to its most formal. Oh, great. He kept his gaze fixed on the doorway, waiting.

CHAPTER 17

At last, Maya entered, her steps hesitant, her arms wrapped around herself as if she were cold. The dark circles under her eyes emphasized her paleness. Her gaze latched onto his, burned with unspoken feelings, deep and intense.

He held out a hand to her. I have missed you, my heart.

And I you. She grasped his hand with her own, pressed it to her face, kissed his palm. Her touch felt so right. He wanted more. He wanted all these people gone so he could touch and kiss Maya all over.

Then a regally dressed woman entered the room. She looked like an older version of Maya. "Well, we haven't had so much excitement for a while," she said. "I, Bayatri, the queen of the water djinns, owe you earth djinns many thanks for taking care of my daughter Maya."

She paused and took a deep breath. "Welcome. I'm happy to say, both our children have survived the worst."

King Dar Zammen stepped forward, his gait stiff. "The Djinns of the Earth owe you many thanks for helping us on the battlefield, for working so hard to save our heir."

Bayatri inclined her head in gracious acknowledgement. "We were close and did what we could."

Ara pushed out from behind her father and Jazz and rushed to Askhay and Maya. She hugged them both. "I'm so glad we got there in time."

Akshay ruffled her hair. "What are you doing here, little bird?"

A crimson blush stained Ara's face as she giggled. "I was worried about Maya and sneaked down to her cell to see her early in the morning," she said. "But I saw Queen Umber and her servant there, so I hid in the shadows and watched them."

Akshay cast a worried glance at Jazz. "I'm sorry about your mother."

Jazz shook his head. "S-she…it's hard to grasp that she tried to kill you so I could have the throne." He swallowed. "I'm the one who's sorry, brother."

"I followed them for a bit, and then ran and told Father," Ara finished.

The king picked up the story again. "We were already on our way here, when we got the water djinns' message." He turned stiffly toward the water king and queen. "I had blamed the water djinns for this disaster, but I was wrong. I was betrayed by my own queen."

Bayatri nodded. "There have always been bad feelings and misunderstandings between us, as is wont to happen between two neighboring countries wrangling to get the best deal."

"Of course, Liana's betrayal of her lawfully wedded husband made matters worse," King Dar Zammen added.

The old healer started, her thin form straightened. "You're mistaken," she said. "She married your father in good faith, but he wasn't strong enough to stand up to his family. They used her water powers without care. They were destroying the earth's balance and killing my sister."

"Water djinns can replenish their powers."

"If given time and opportunity," the healer said. "A husband should look out for and care for his wife. Your father failed to do so and killed any love she'd ever had for him."

The king stood, arms folded, chin out. "How are you going to explain her lover?"

"He was a hero," the queen interjected. "The earth djinns had cut Liana away from all contact with us—"

"Once a woman marries, she belongs to her husband's people according to custom and protocol." The king squared his shoulders and firmed his stance.

Bayatri whipped him a cutting glance. "Not ours. Dirk Nightingale used his mage powers to bring her here, and then he helped us keep you all out of our lives. His powers mingled with ours, and it's that strength that helps us fight you and other invaders off to this day."

Ideas gelled in Akshay's mind. Human magic had infused and changed the water djinns' powers. That explained the impenetrable underground walls the moles had encountered.

His father kneaded his temple. "All we want is water to survive."

"We give you enough for survival."

The king stomped up to her. "And not a drop more."

"We don't want you to have so much that you build an army and decide to take over the world."

"We wouldn't do that," the king rumbled.

"Really? History proves otherwise," The queen said, turning away. "You'd better take your son and leave. We have done all we will do for him."

The words pierced Akshay like the assassin swords, stabbed at his heart over and over. Maya's hand gripped his tighter. He pushed himself up in bed, ready to intervene. But before he could get a word out, his father spoke.

"Fine, we will take Maya and Akshay and leave by noon."

Denidra stepped up to the king, all lithe grace and sharp weapons. "Maya is not going anywhere with you."

Akshay's gaze darted about the room as tall water djinns, armed and dressed in silver armor, emerged from the crowd. They flanked all the key earth djinns in the room, relaxed but ready, with hands resting on the hilt of their swords.

His father shook with rage, did what he always did when pushed. Pushed back. "Why the hell not? She's carrying my grandson, and she will be queen one day."

"A queen of the earth djinns is little more than a slave," Bayatri's voice sliced through the room. "My daughter is not going to your court to be mistreated."

"We are not uncivilized boors, we do not mistreat our women." King Dar Zammen pulled in a deep breath. "Our mothers, wives and daughters are respected and protected. They have voice in not only the running of the palace, but also in court." He squared his shoulders. "We do not owe you any explanation. Maya is carrying a future earth king and she is going with us."

A rumble cracked the air as the building shook, and startled cries rang out as djinns stumbled against one another. Once everything settled, the king brushed dust off his cuff. "Don't push me. Earth djinns have powers here too."

Quick as a silver fish in water, Denidra had her sword unsheathed and at the king's throat. "The baby is our future also. Maya stays."

Hell. Akshay grimaced. Could things go any worse? "Enough!"

When all eyes turned toward him and Maya, he raised her hand to his lips and placed a soft kiss on the back. "None of you have a say in this," he said. "Maya and I need to talk and decide what our plans are."

Grandmother's eyes almost bugged out. "But we are the elders!"

"And we respect you as elders," Maya said. "However, a shared life would be between Akshay and me, so it is our decision."

"But—"

"This is not up for discussion." Maya leaned back into him, hands still joined, and they stared down the room. The two of them against the rest of their crazy families.

No one moved, so Akshay cleared his throat. "We need to discuss this alone."

His words galvanized djinns into action. Grumbles and whispers filled the air as djinns trickled out of the room. He looked at Maya. "I'd really like to get out into the fresh air."

"Sounds good." Maya pulled aside a healer and had a whispered conference. Within moments, the healer brought them a wheeled chair and helped Akshay in.

"Thank you." Maya wheeled him to the double glass doors and out onto the balcony.

Akshay smiled as he pulled in a breath of sun-warmed air. They stared in silence at the lush green meadow spilling beneath them, dotted with wildflowers. So much like the plain in front of Nijhoom forest.

Maya touched his shoulders, rubbed and warmed them. Just a casual, caring touch without any expectations. A simple touch seeking to comfort. He looked up at her and smiled.

She bent down and brushed her lips across his. "Woohoo! We escaped."

He grinned and looked back again at the wildflowers. So many colors and shapes, so much life. "The battlefield was covered in flowers like these," he said. "But when I first saw it, the plain was barren. What changed it?"

Maya leaned on his shoulders, sighed. "Our joined essences—from the water djinns and earth djinns who died that day—fed the earth, gave birth to new life."

"Earth and water together can accomplish much." He covered one of her hands with his, stroked his thumb across the soft skin at her wrist. A cheerful yellow butterfly danced by them.

He listened to the birds twittering as another, more important question formed in his mind. "I need to know, was your time among the earth djinns totally terrible?"

"The cell and the escape would fit that description," she said. "But the rest of it...I saw parts of your land that were eye-opening and beautiful. Spending time with you, I discovered things about myself I never knew."

His eyes burned with tears as he swallowed past the lump in his throat. "And you know that as a woman, my queen, you will have a cherished and honored place in the court like my mother?"

She slipped her hand from his and came around the front, squatted down so she looked him in the eyes. "I have lied to you enough and for that I apologize, and I will lie to you no more," she said. "I wouldn't want a daughter of mine hidden away for her protection, cherished yet not celebrated."

"What do you mean?"

"Do you remember the fruit tree dispute between two neighbors?"

He nodded.

"Who came up with the solution in the end?"

"My queen mother," he said, a smile flickered across his face. "See, women have a voice. She's bossing all of us all the time."

Maya returned a small smile, her eyes warm with love and sadness. "It was Ara. She is wise beyond her years."

He stared at her, stunned. "Little bird?"

"Who do you think we really owe our lives to, whose intervention truly saved us?"

He closed his eyes, pressing back the pain her truthful words caused him. How the hell had he been so blind, so wrapped up in his own worries not to notice his sister suffocating under protocol? Heat swarmed up his neck and face. "Ara."

"She is wise, courageous and resourceful, but could she ever rule Bhramadesh, or sit on the council?" Maya's voice hitched. "Why not?"

He opened his eyes, stared fiercely into her gaze. "You're right. It isn't fair, and I understand why you wouldn't want to have our baby in Bhramadesh."

Akshay released a deep breath. "What if I was willing to walk away from the crown? What if I wanted to stay right here with you?" His voice shook. "Could you accept me then?"

In reply, she kissed him. A long, sweet drawn out kiss. "You once told me as crown prince you have to take care of your people, and that's the man I love," she said. "Would you be able to walk away from Ara and the earth djinns without even trying to fix things?"

"You're right. Things need to change." Unshed tears glittered in his eyes. "But change will take time, and I need to work from within. I understand why we can't be together, why you will not marry me."

"I don't remember saying I wouldn't."

He drank her dear face in, searched it for any hint of a joke. "You would?" he asked. "Even after seeing what you have seen, even after Liana's story?"

She nodded.

"Why?"

"Because I love you and I trust you."

He pulled her into his lap and kissed her, hard and desperate. He drank her in, reveling in her clean rain scent. He thanked the Creator for her and this moment, for the first time he'd seen her and every minute in between. He kissed Maya and found home.

After a long moment, they untangled themselves. "So you're saying yes?"

"Yes."

He gave her a gentle kiss. "Thank you."

She giggled. "You know as soon as we tell them, they'll be throwing a feast and marrying us off."

"Well then, we should definitely make them wait."
He settled back into the chair and she snuggled into
him.

She rubbed her still-flat tummy. "You have a plan."

"We'll get married before the baby comes, but I'm
thinking a long engagement with lots of trips back and
forth, and lots of joint projects," he said. "Really force
them to get to know each other."

She laughed. "A wise man once told me good things
come to those who wait."

"And he was right." He kissed her again and
everything felt right, full of new promises. She had
changed him and he had changed her. Together they
created a new life. And together they would create a
new world. A better one, for their children and their
children's children.

A world changed with patience and strategy, but
mostly love.

###

ABOUT MINA

Mina Khan is a Texas-based writer and food enthusiast. She daydreams of hunky paranormal heroes, magic, mayhem and mischief and writes them down as stories. Between stories, she teaches culinary classes and writes for her local newspaper. Other than that, she's raising a family of two children, two cats, two dogs and a husband.

She grew up in Bangladesh on stories of djinns, ghosts and monsters. These childhood fancies now color her fiction. Her debut novella, THE DJINN'S DILEMMA was published November 2011. This second novella, A TALE OF TWO DJINNS, was released March 2012.

She loves hearing from readers.

You can find her at:
Facebook Author Page:
https://www.facebook.com/Mina.Khan.Author
Blog: http://minakhan.blogspot.com/
Twitter: http://twitter.com/SpiceBites